WHEN
YOU
LEAVE
I
DISAPPEAR

WHEN
YOU
LEAVE
I
DISAPPEAR

A NOVELLA

DAVID NIALL WILSON

SHORTWAVE

Cover art and interior design by Alan Lastufka.

First Edition published August 2024.

10 9 8 7 6 5 4 3 2 1

ISBN 978-1-959565-38-3 (Paperback)
ISBN 978-1-959565-39-0 (eBook)

To Alan Lastufka, who told me what he wanted this book to be about and was still fully on board when it turned out to be something else. . .

CHAPTER ONE

Andrea Simmons closed her laptop, pressed down on the lid until the screen bowed from the pressure, and screamed at the top of her lungs. Beating the desk, she tried to rip at the smooth wooden surface with her nails, but only succeeded in breaking two and cracking a third. On the screen was her latest post, announcing the release of *Imagine Us in Heaven*, the eighth romantic suspense novel featuring Teresa Vincent, investigative journalist with a steamy past. It had 4,987 likes and had been shared nearly that many times. Preorders were through the roof, and reviews already projected it as a bestseller—one of the books of the year on a wide variety of sites. Andrea knew it was the saddest piece of crap she'd ever attached her name to, and knowing that her agent, Sylvia, gushing over the advance reviews, would be calling for the next in the series, made her stomach clench as if she'd been punched.

And it wasn't the story. It wasn't the characters. It just felt disconnected, like something she'd written with no investment at all. She had always loved the characters. The twists and turns of the plots, the relationships, and the backstories. But, somewhere in the pages of this book, she'd lost that connection, and now she couldn't remember what it had been like. Had it ever really been there, or was she just fooling herself?

There was a knock on the door of her office. She wanted to scream again, to tell whoever was there to fuck off and leave her alone, but she knew it was Jenifer. There was no way she could take this out on Jen; all this was on her. The famous author, horrified by the success of her own work, and unable to stop the relentless progress of her literary bullshit train. Every new addition to the series had brought more stress, more demands from her agent, editor, reviewers, and fans. The fans who had, up until this moment, been her companions in that other world, sharing the fantasies she felt slipping away. She'd forgotten her dreams and felt destined to be remembered for a short time, for work that never mattered on any level deeper than momentary escape, and then forgotten. She'd been living two lives, one in a romantic adventure land and the other one lost in a hot wash of frustration. Now one of them seemed to have vanished.

"Go away," she said. Not loud enough.

The knocking continued.

"Fuck," she said. After a moment, she added, "Come in."

The door opened. She felt the shift in air pressure, heard the soft tread of slippered feet. She didn't look up, even when she felt Jen's hands on her shoulders, working at her taut muscles and trying to pry loose the anger.

"Too loud?" she asked.

"What's wrong?"

Andrea shook her head. No answer. Her chair was pulled back slowly, and she allowed it. Jen slipped between her and the computer, hit the power button and brought the screen back to life. Jen scrolled through the comments on the post, hesitating now and then to take in details.

"*Publishers Weekly* says it's your best yet," Jen said. She kept her voice steady, but Andrea caught the subtle humor. "A rare talent."

Andrea pushed back, turned, and stood. "I can't do it anymore," she said. "I can't sit through another round of talk shows, book clubs, vapid reviews from people who wouldn't know a good book if I hit them in the head with it. Believe me, in my mind I have done that so many times I'm afraid I'll wake up on air and realize it finally happened. I just can't."

"Maybe it's time to pull a James Patterson," Jen said. "Who would know? We could slip off to an island paradise and just watch the dollar signs flip. You've said it before; almost anyone could write this."

Andrea dropped her head into her hands and let out a breath so deep it sounded like leaking steam.

"I never really meant it like that; I don't want to quit," she said at last. "I want what I write to feel important. I want to prove that it's not just the series, and the name and 'brand' selling books. When I created Teresa Vincent, I was invested in her. When I wrote those early books, it was as if I stepped into her world, felt her pain, shared her victories. What if all of that was just me indulging myself? I mean, what if I *never* had any talent? What if I hit the right thing on the desk of an agent and it was all a cosmic accident? Would any of those readers recognize it if someone else wrote the books? Especially this one? I'm afraid of that answer. I want to know, but the idea of knowing terrifies me."

"Ten million books sold and imposter syndrome?"

"Maybe. I don't know. I just want to do something," Andrea waved her hand at the computer screen, "not *this*."

"It's not like you need the money," Jen said. "If you don't want to do the next book, just tell them. A year off? Six months? Blackmail them into publishing whatever you do in the meantime under a pseudonym? You don't have to work another day to be comfortable for the rest of your life."

"But I'm not. Comfortable, I mean. I'm going slowly crazy. It's as if there is nothing left of what I set out to be, just a 'Stepford Wives' word-producing automaton. I'm going to ask for that break, to do something different. Is it weird to need validation when your face pops up on digital billboards in Times Square every time a new book comes out? And if I do stop, what about those characters? What about the world I've invested so much of my adult life in?"

"Of course, it's weird," Jen said, "but what's wrong with weird? You coming to bed?"

"In a while. I'm going to do some surfing, maybe some research. I need to find some sort of answer to this. I won't be too long. Probably."

"I could do it, you know," Jen said. "Write those books for them, I mean. I've edited them all. I've brainstormed them with you. . . it might even be fun."

Andrea fell silent for a moment.

"That might feel even weirder than having someone else do it. What if you were the one with the ideas, and the talent, and I've just been hitting the keys?"

"I thought you didn't care about the reviews and the fame."

Andrea frowned, then stuck out her tongue.

Jen laughed and kissed her on the top of her head.

"I won't wait up," she said.

Andrea nodded, but she was already gone, barely aware of the transition. Jen closed the door as quietly as she could.

* * *

Andrea glared at her computer screen and tried to come up with a search term that would inspire her. She avoided anything that might lead her back to romantic suspense, but she had no idea what she was looking for. She'd read a wide variety of books by other authors, biographies, books *about* writing, novels, collections, horror, science fiction, and fantasy. She'd even found some fan fiction sites that intrigued her over the years, but she knew they weren't what she was after – what she needed. There were fan fiction sites writing about Teresa Vincent. She needed something absolutely unique.

She searched social media for "cutting edge" authors. She looked for trends. She read free stories on a dozen online markets. Nothing felt real. Nothing touched her. Then, just before clicking in on the thirteenth online story, the words "writers prompt" caught her attention. The story she'd been about to read had been inspired by someone else's post. A snippet of prose, or an image, a plot twist, something that unlocked the words and allowed them to flow freely.

She closed all but her browser window which was waiting for a new search. She typed quickly.

My writing prompts

The screen filled instantly with thousands of hits, most of which said "does not include 'my'" – with a prompt to search *only* for the exact phrase. She clicked the only link. That web page was titled (ironically) "My Writing prompts."

She waited as the site loaded. There was the usual warning about collecting cookies, which she accepted. The screen flickered, and a simple form appeared in the center of a black screen.

LOGIN – or CREATE ACCOUNT?

She clicked create account and a new screen appeared. She frowned. There were none of the usual suspects among the fields she was presented. No username. No password.

First question: Are you a talented writer?

There was a button for YES. There were no other choices. She hesitated over the YES. A blue circle appeared across the black background. The blue began to disappear at the top, spinning clockwise around the circle and leaving only the black. She wanted to press the button on her mouse and move to the next screen, but she was paralyzed. Was she a talented writer? What did she have to show that would prove it? The Teresa Vincent novels? The short stories in literary magazines she'd written in college that made her cringe every time she re-read them? The bits and pieces of things she'd collected and recorded in journals that had never gotten past the point of ideas? She blinked and realized the blue had completely disappeared. She was about to hit the back key and return to the main screen, thinking it had simply timed out, when the screen shifted again.

"ENTER SAMPLE" was at the top of the screen.

Beneath that in smaller type, "Write something that is real. Write what you want to say to the world."

Then there was a large blank text box. Andrea stared at it. She'd come to the site to get prompts, not provide them. She felt unprepared and oddly vulnerable. Her fingers found the keys, and she began typing the first thing that came to mind. "Alexis Jones was a tall, thin woman with jet black hair and an icy smile."

The words disappeared from the screen. Another circle, larger than the first one, appeared to the right of the text box. This one was white, but began slowly turning red, moving steadily around from the top like the first. Andrea closed her eyes, flashed back to the first question, then to the review of *Imagine Us in Heaven*, and began to write.

* * *

Every face you see is a mask and every face you present to the world is also a mask. Some people are experts at shifting from one to the next. The face they show you won't be the same as the one

    your husband or wife sees. They navigate rooms, features flickering from one countenance to another so quickly it's seamless and impossible to track.

Most people are not so adept. Their masks will linger and give away secrets. Features slip into place that present them to the world in ways that don't feel real, that are paper-thin and fragile enough to blow away in a gust of wind. Those are the masks you cherish, patching them and molding them until they solidify. Who you believe you are or want the world to buy into. Masks can protect you, but they crack. If you wear them too long, you can forget what's important. Masks aren't protection, they're a prison, and every face is a mask.

There are more dangerous masks. There are more inescapable prisons. These are created for you by others, molded around your features and your words, creating something you have no control over. The more who see and accept that face, the harder it becomes to remove. You wear it in public. No matter how hard you try, it seeps into your private life, shows itself to friends and colleagues, replacing your features and stealing your identity. Imposter syndrome is a very simple disorder when you consider how many imposters you might actually be.

If you want to change the world, you have to break them all. The most terrifying face you can present to the world is the one that hurts the most, the one that burns in the sun and faces the world unprotected. These are the faces of artists, writers, creators. They are the faces that will be remembered far beyond death. They are the faces that lead to madness, or greatness, or both.

The mask I wear is killing me. I have to break it. I have to destroy it, but I am afraid. It's a face the world loves. What if, after it's broken, what's left isn't enough? What if I'm not enough?

* * *

Andrea lifted her fingers from the keys and stared at the screen. What she'd written had come from somewhere deep inside. From her frustration with her career, her hatred of the work she was doing, combined with her absolute fear of disappointing her fans, her editor, or losing touch with the world she'd created. What would result if they suspected how she felt, or even worse, how she regarded their adoration. If she was an imposter, and what she wrote was crap, what did it say about the millions of readers who snapped up every title as soon as it hit the shelf? Or the book clubs full of wine tastings, blog tours, and book reviewers who raved and promoted her?

The screen shifted. There was no button to submit the work, and no way to know how the website had known that what she had written first was bullshit or seemed to have known. Why it had reacted to what she'd just typed, but not to what she'd entered before. No explanation for the circle that appeared, the timer calling her bluff. Like someone was watching, reading, and reacting as she typed, which was totally creepy, nearly impossible, and somehow darkly inspiring.

The screen went dark, then blinked back to life.

ACCOUNT CREATED
PRESS ENTER FOR PROMPT

* * *

Andrea pressed the enter key, and a line of text appeared on the screen. She read it, then read it again. The screen went blank.

She froze. Waited. Nothing. Then a second line of text appeared.

SUCCESSFULLY LOGGED OFF. PROMPT VALID FOR TWENTY-FOUR HOURS.

The prompt. What had it said? She'd read it, but. . . then she knew.

"The first thing you ever wanted to write. The first thing you ever wrote."

She opened a new document and quickly typed out the words. Then she sat back, and she stared. What kind of prompt was this? How was this supposed to help? The first thing?

She closed her eyes and a scene flashed into sharp focus. It was her ninth grade English Composition class. She was planted firmly in the front row, surrounded by whispering, bored classmates. Mrs. Anderson, the teacher, was talking, and Andrea was trying her best to hear every word.

They were getting their first creative writing assignment. Everything up to that point had been essays, or book reports. This was different. They were supposed to write about something that mattered to them, something important. It didn't matter to her that the others didn't care, this was what she'd been waiting for. Her bookshelves at home overflowed with books, Nancy Drew, Alfred Hitchcock, a set of classics her father had given her with *Anne of Green Gables, Treasure Island,* others. Andrea had wanted to be a writer since she'd learned to put one word next to another. She had notebooks full of ideas, poems, snippets of stories, and ideas, but no one knew. Not her mother, not even her father, who she believed would be proud.

Because what if she couldn't do it? What if she could read and dissolve into the stories that others wrote, but her own imagination fell short? What if the things that fascinated her just made people laugh at her, or ignore her?

And what mattered? What *really* mattered? She knew what she wanted to write about. She wanted to write about books. She wanted to find a way to make her classmates laugh, those who watched TV, played video games, and only read things they absolutely had to for class. They'd never understand, probably wouldn't even listen if she had to read the paper out loud.

She'd decided to ask her only real friend, Robin Orestad, about it. Robin would laugh at her for spending so much time worrying over a homework assignment, but if she didn't think the idea was too weird, Andrea thought she might find the courage to write it. Maybe she *was* overthinking it, and everything would be fine.

Of course, things had not worked out that way. At first, Robin wasn't even interested enough to talk about it, but when she saw how serious Andrea was, how miserable it was making her, her friend had come around.

"You can't write about *that*," Robin said. "No one reads. . . not really. If you don't want even more people to think you're weird, you need to make them think something else is important."

"Like?"

"Like boys," Robin said. "Or dancing, or—I don't know—aren't there any bands you like that people would have heard of? Romance. My mom is the only one I know who reads. She has piles of romance novels beside her chair in a basket. She has them sent to her, you know, like a subscription? And she buys them in Walmart. . . all the covers seem kind of the same. I've checked a few of them out. Let's just say my dad would *not* be happy if he knew what they were about. Or maybe he does. . . grownups are weird. But you have to write about things that *matter*."

Something inside had snapped. Nothing changed about what mattered to Andrea, but her perspective on the assignment, the world, her friend? Never the same again. She saw that there was an easier road. People read what they want to read, listen to what they want to, and the simplest road to success was to give them what they wanted.

She spent two days outlining a paper explaining how music was important to her because of the way it touched people. If you were sad, you heard sad songs and could believe the lyrics were written about you. If you were in love, the love songs spoke to your heart, and if you needed a party, it was only an album away. All of it was true, of course, but there was one thing that was absolutely not true. It wasn't important to Andrea. Not in the way the assignment suggested. The fact that none of the other essays turned in were any deeper or more heartfelt had not changed the message. Her paper had garnered an A+. Some of the other students, mostly girls, had actually told her she'd touched them with the words, that music was exactly like that.

And of course, they were right. Music affected Andrea the same way, but it wasn't the music that was important to her, it was her connection to the music. The same was true of books, but she had no intention of creating music. She wanted to see her name on the covers of books. There were so many stories she wanted to tell, and every day there were more. Things that were important. To her. She had never told them. Not one. Except to Jen, and that so many years beyond the memory, she was lost in what felt like a different world. Jen was one of those things now, but there were levels and depths where her thoughts walked alone.

Her bookshelves were filled with the hardcover and paperback editions of her twenty-two novels, and the two collections of her short fiction that had been published in romance magazines and online promotional releases. Not a single one of them mattered to her. She'd dropped bits and pieces of her life into a few of them, but the resolutions, and the romantic bits, had never resonated. She'd stolen them from popular music, from Hallmark movies, and conversations with friends. She'd had relationships, none of them serious, but she'd built them into epic love stories she could tap into, like listening to endless pop radio nonsense for references that fit. She was a master puzzle-maker with a flair for adventure.

It had been so long since she'd thought about writing anything else, and what she wrote worked. That was the real problem. She'd achieved everything in the universe that she'd thought she wanted. Her early novels had caught the attention of publishers, and once she'd created Teresa Vincent and shared that universe with the world, there had been no turning back. The worst of it was that it had happened without her even noticing. Until this night, until she'd seen the prompt, she hadn't even been fully aware.

The first thing she'd written had been a lie, but the first thing she'd wanted to write would have changed her life. Could it still? She'd read so many more books, lived vicariously through so many stories.

She turned back to her laptop and began to type. She tried to remember the books she'd been reading when that long ago assignment had been handed out. She tried to dip deep for the sense of wonder, the magic that had drawn her into those stories. She hadn't typed two sentences before her fingers slowed, and then stopped, resting nervously on the keys. That story, whatever it might have become, was gone. The books that had filled her world felt empty and trite.

Like her life. Like her *own* work made her feel. They might have mattered when she was young or even changed her life, but they were lost to her, and they were no longer a part of what mattered.

What mattered were words. When she thought of the books, stories, relationships, reviews, agents, editors, and fans, they existed for her in a kaleidoscopic swirl of words. Stories and books were important, but only if the words mattered. Only if they were able to affect change, to reach people and make a difference.

It was like a moonshine still, or alchemy. You took a book, or an idea, a conversation or even the record of a life, created in words, and reduced it. You found the essence and cherished it. Except, no one did. The stories, articles, books, and movies were only more masks. Words had to cut, twist, and mold things to a new reality. They needed to change the world.

She deleted the nonsense she had typed about books and began to write.

"THE WORD"

In the beginning there was the Word. The Word was with God, and the Word was God, or something like that. We'll never really know for sure, will we? Once there was more than one word, the obfuscation began. Clara knew that was the only gospel that mattered, so when she picked up her journal and added an entry, it was the one thing in her day that got her total attention. There were no wasted words, and there were no half-truths. If the book ever got into the hands of friends, family, or co-workers, her entire world would shift on its shaky axis of lies, half-truths, and creative disguise. The risk was necessary. What held her together was recording the things she did, encountered, loved, and hated, and doing so with as few words as possible, all of them accurate.

* * *

The morning was foggy. I could barely make out the mailbox by the street. A single car passed. Mrs. Multinerry waved to the driver, but she didn't know him. She waves at every car. One day a mass murderer may visit the neighborhood and that wave could be what saves our lives. Or dooms us.

Everyone's trash was out for pick-up except for Sam Burnett's. The truck was already on our block, waking babies and dogs with its banging, crashing, whistling cacophony of brakes and hydraulics when Sam wheeled his can out to meet them. The minute it was empty, he rolled it back around the side of the house and sealed it in its enclosure. Sam didn't want people to know what's in the garbage or didn't care that we are all aware of this.

I took delivery of groceries at ten and placed my bills in the mailbox. There were three deliveries on the porch. I didn't answer the door but brought the packages in as quickly as possible. Sam isn't the only person who believes their personal life should be private.

One package contained two wireless cameras. I added them to my security system and put them inconspicuously in windows facing two neighbors' homes. Tim Johnson and Bailey Lawrence have been challenging the balance. The neighborhood depends on privacy and seclusion for its dynamic. We are not friends. Barely on speaking terms, and then only when the words are meaningless and easily forgotten. Never when they matter.

Tim and Bailey have forgotten the rules. More likely, they never understood them. Tim has strangers coming and going, pulling in and out of his driveway at all hours, lights on and music too loud after nine p.m. His garbage can, unlike Sam's, is rolled in next to the wall of his garage. It often overflows. Garbage has actually blown from his yard into his neighbors'. It will be dealt with, of course. There are consequences.

Bailey has been working late nights in his back yard. He thinks I don't see. There is a tarp he pulls from one side of his fence to the other when the sun goes down. He uses shaded lights. I can't hear anything from my window, and I would never cross into another yard. There are borders. Bailey is doing something improper, but on his own grounds. Rules matter. Borders are sacred.

The cameras are motion-detecting. They will catch pieces of the puzzle. The second package I received requires more finesse. It contained two directional microphones, also wireless. If someone sees the cameras, they will assume it's part of a security system. The microphones are different. Intrusive. In a very private neighborhood, they risk the balance. Necessary risk.

The third package can wait.

* * *

The lights were on at Tim Johnson's house, and the driveway was full. Inside, music throbbed, an industrial dance track. No words, just backbeat and bass. Sometimes the strangers arriving brought their own overblown sound systems, they parked, and the discordant music flowed over and around them, making them a single lighted, throbbing whole. Men and women were sucked through the door like a portal.

Clara's camera caught it all. The microphone had been muted. Even the powerful directional capability of the system was battered to submission by the music. Nothing was recorded, but there was time. The video was high resolution and it caught faces, interactions, gestures, and trysts. There was more than music controlling Johnson's house, and any time reality, logic, and judgment are sacrificed, chinks appear in the armor. People were making mistakes, and they were being recorded.

Things changed hands. Couples were caught in intimate moments. Couples whose individual members were known. Many of them were not supposed to be together at all, let alone in public. Facial recognition and a thorough understanding of search engines and social media helped Clara fill in the blanks. The music was a problem. Without the words, there wasn't enough. Video was gold... but the words. There was no backing off from the words. In the beginning there was the word.

Around eleven, the music lowered in volume, and by midnight, it had faded to silence. There were still several vehicles in the driveway. The directional microphones went live, and Clara went to bed. She didn't need to be awake to hear the details, just needed them to be recorded.

* * *

Tim Johnson paid no attention to his neighbors. None of them had the balls to complain about his parties, and that was just how he liked it. The gatherings were smokescreens for his work. Everyone had a good time. He made a little on the side off of the drugs, but it was all carefully designed to camouflage the serious business being conducted.

He always had a drink in his hand, but he never drank. He hated the very idea of being impaired, and it might have proven suicidal, all things considered. He sat, his full glass on a coaster beside him, watching the others come and go, letting the music wash over him. The night's guest list had been carefully curated. The proper palms had been greased, and there would be no interference from local law enforcement. He'd seen his neighbor—Celia? Cora?—placing her cameras, and he knew one of them faced his driveway. He'd nearly waved to let her know, but held back.

Nothing important would be recorded, but there was the possibility that a lot of distractions would. He had no illusions about his guests. They were empty-headed rich kids with their parents' credit cards and nothing better to do. He'd lured them in with the music, the promise of drugs, and like-minded drones to make a party of it. All smoke and mirrors, except one.

He glanced down the street to Bailey Lawrence's place. The lights were out, but Tim knew the tarp was up, and work was underway. It was pretty remarkable what Bailey had done. Even more so what he *could* do.

The two of them were a match made somewhere, but absolutely not in Heaven.

The rest of the neighborhood was populated by odd recluses. Tim was vaguely aware of Sam Burnett. He'd wondered what the guy was hiding in that trash he was so careful not to let anyone see. Tim might have gone over to find out or sent one of his party crowd on a dare, but there were cameras everywhere. He had no doubt there was a grid, carefully annotated, with all the transgressions each strange old bird counted worthy of recording.

The screech of tires and a momentary shift in the music announced yet another arrival. Tim lifted his glass and watched the door. An almost cruelly thin, fancifully made-up couple entered. He allowed himself a single shake of his hand, hearing the ice cubes clink. His expression never changed, but his target was acquired.

He placed the glass on his kitchen counter. He drew his phone from his pocket and opened an encrypted text window. He typed a single X and hit send, then closed the app, locked his phone, and slid it back into his pocket. Game on.

* * *

Bailey heard the chirp of a text message hitting his phone and glanced up from his work. His home's previous owner had been in the process of installing an inground pool. The neighborhood had shut them down, and part of the agreement Bailey had signed with the HOA required him to fill it in and replace the lawn. Being something of an overachiever, he'd done much, much more.

He knew that the delivery of any significant construction materials would splash across his nosy neighbors' radar, so he'd improvised. He'd brought it all home, one load at a time in the back of his truck, carefully covered with a hard-shell casing. Then he moved it to his garage, and at night, from the garage to the open maw of the ill-fated pool.

First, bags of concrete and strong mortar. Then posts and beams. He'd had to hurry in those early days. The illusion came first, then the real work could begin. He'd laid in a foundation, then roofed it over near the surface of the yard. He'd sealed that with plastic and covered it all in sod. Phase One had left him with a fire pit covering a set of stairs leading downward, and one of the greenest, smoothest lawns in all the neighborhood's backyards.

It was easy enough to mask the construction with music, timing nail gun blasts to staccato drumbeats, working patiently. As much fabrication, cutting, and shaping as possible was done in a remote workshop, then hauled in, one truckload at a time, and always at five thirty. He timed it so it seemed like he was returning from the day job they all believed he held. No one really cared. A few mumbled sentences about the office, the grind, and they were off to their own little worlds, filing him away as a drudge who liked his music a little too loud.

Roll forward three months and things were a lot more sophisticated. The interior of the bunker had been insulated for sound. The walls were lined with metal cages set into the walls. Each was a tiny pod. That's what he called them after he saw something similar in a documentary on tiny houses. He'd tapped into the water and sewer lines. Each had a sink, a very basic camper-style toilet, a reclining "gamer" style chair that could double for a bed if you were tired enough. He had a slot for safely passing objects like food, books, whatever. No one stayed long. He wasn't a collector, after all. He was a broker.

The rooms were also set up so he could close vents and pump in gas. He took no chances with his charges. They were young, often intelligent, and each very valuable to someone. Bailey didn't talk with them, didn't know more than their names. Orders came in, were transferred to him. He procured and delivered. All business, smooth and simple. It would have bothered him, but Bailey knew those behind it all, and he believed that whatever he was a part of was a positive thing. His childhood and his escape from that world anchored that belief.

Unlike Tim, he paid no attention to the neighbors, believing the more he watched them or worried over them, it would undermine his routines. He couldn't afford to be paranoid. He didn't know about Clara and her cameras, or the directional microphones. Even if he'd known, he probably wouldn't have paid attention. There was no way the microphone could pick up any sound, and there was nothing for a camera to see except grass. He'd replaced the temporary stairway entrance with a short tunnel from his garage.

The text was from Tim. Time to retrieve and store. One day, then delivery. Smooth and simple. He responded with a simple thumbs-up emoji and exited through the tunnel to his truck. He never walked across the street. He never said a word to Tim or spoke with him in public. Text only, except when making a pickup. Backing out of his garage, he headed out of the neighborhood and into the city. Ten minutes later he swung back in from the opposite end of the street and nosed the big Ford in among the BMWs and Camaros still surrounding Tim's party. The music caused the truck to vibrate, as if he'd parked on the fabric of a sub-woofer.

He didn't enter through the front door. Instead, he slipped around the side of the house, opened the gate in the wooden privacy fence, and stepped into the backyard. There were couples in all the corners, some making out, others dancing slowly to the music. One kid in Gucci sneakers had passed out with his shoulders leaning on the fence, a half-full Heineken tipped and spilling into the grass beside him.

Bailey memorized where they all stood, and what they were doing, but didn't speak or make eye contact. Instead, he walked in the door to the back of the kitchen, grabbed a beer someone had left on the counter, and made his way slowly down the hallway to the bedrooms in the rear. He knew Tim would be waiting. They just had to secure the package and make the transfer to the truck without attracting any attention. Another routine. The privileged crowd was consumed by itself. Nothing peripheral mattered, and the party was winding down. Couples were slipping off and finding quiet corners or leaving. Those without partners were scanning the remnants, looking for something new, or different, or available.

No one would see. No one would care. Tim would deal with the car. Bailey got the product. He knocked on the last door on the left, then entered and closed it behind him.

The sound of the lock clicking into place was lost in the music.

* * *

Clara rose early. She made coffee, retrieved her newspaper, set her laptop up on the kitchen table, and settled in. First, she played the footage from Tim Johnson's home. She set the playback at one and a half speed. Most of it was simple comings and goings. The microphone was muted through one in the morning. She had a notebook beside her coffee cup, and jotted observations now and then. Mostly she watched. She had started recording when the driveway began filling up. The music had died down around one thirty and she'd activated the microphone, but it was another half hour before things fell silent.

She paused the video when a vehicle that seemed out of place slid in beside a BMW. A truck it only took her a moment to place. Bailey? She slowed the playback and watched the man slip around the side of the house toward the backyard and out of sight.

She turned up the audio. The music was still too loud to make out any conversations, so she turned it back down and concentrated on the truck. About ten minutes later, Bailey exited the front door. Beside him, a young man, and a girl with a weird mohawk that dangled down to cover one eye, staggered under the weight of a second young man, an arm over either of their shoulders. They half-dragged, half carried him to the truck and lifted him into the passenger seat with Bailey's help. The door was closed, and the truck pulled out, but did not turn toward Bailey's house a block away. It turned in the opposite direction and disappeared from sight.

Clara paused the video. She toggled to the camera that had been trained on Bailey's house and fast-forwarded to the matching timestamp. She hit play and watched. Less than ten minutes later, Bailey's truck approached from the far end of the street and turned into his drive. When he hesitated to open the garage door, she paused the playback. It was impossible to make out features, but there was someone in the passenger seat.

The truck disappeared into the garage. Clara

turned up the microphone, but after the engine died, there was only the sound of the truck's doors opening, and then a softer click that must have been another door closing behind them. After that, very literally, nothing.

Clara flipped back to Tim's feed and fast forwarded until all the vehicles were gone. It was quiet, but she heard the clink of a glass. A soft thud that could have been a refrigerator door closing. Footsteps, and then a TV. She returned to Tim's feed. Nothing. Then a car drove by on the street, and she heard wheels whispering over the pavement. There was nothing wrong with the microphone, there was simply nothing to hear.

She ran through the rest of the recording, ignoring Tim's place. Around four o'clock., there was another door opening, and after that, footsteps, water running, a single light came on in what she knew must be Bailey's bedroom. Ten minutes later, the lights went out, and the silence returned.

Clara closed the program, shut down her laptop. She retrieved a bagel from the breadbox in the pantry and dropped it into the toaster. She turned off the coffee pot and put water on to boil. When she was seated at the table once more, the bagel warming her stomach, and a hot cup of mint tea beside her, she opened her journal and began to write.

* * *

Something has changed. A young man was moved from Tim Burnett's party to Bailey's garage. Whoever that was went through a door and disappeared. No sound. Tim made noise as he went to bed, but there was no one else speaking or moving about his home.

Bailey did not pull the tarp across his yard last night. There were no dimmed lights. Whatever he is doing can't be visible because the HOA is about to inspect to be certain he has filled in the unauthorized swimming pool. I feel certain there will be grass. Sam Burnett will be the one to head the inspection, and Sam is sharp. He will be vigilant, but he will also be discreet. There are rules. There are boundaries. If the rules aren't broken, he won't cross the boundary. They will find nothing.

There are records for all of us. The HOA performs a standard background check. Those who have been here longer perform a deeper dive. I will ask Sam for the records on Tim and Bailey. He won't ask why. There are rules, and there are boundaries. The rules say I am privy to the records, the boundaries say he can't question my motive.

Others will be informed of my request. Some of them may request the material as well. They may ask what I have discovered, and, if they do, I'll provide it. Some will know more than I about the possibilities.

Tim and Bailey are new to the neighborhood. Their period of silence is growing short. Soon they will be invited to the HOA or we will move on. Theirs are prime proper-ties. The issue with Tim's garbage is a small one, but an indicator. It could become a problem if it's an attitude and not simply a modifiable behavior. Most behavior can be modified, but some minds cannot. Bailey has broken no rules. His border is safe, so long as no attention is drawn.

"I will send my files to Sam, along with my request for the records, and continue to monitor. Before the end of the week, everyone will be watching and waiting.

It's sunny out today, with only a slight breeze. I will work in my garden and raise the second flag on my mailbox to be sure Sam knows to check for my message, but I know he'll get the alert. Everyone will. It's why I worded it so carefully; the words matter."

* * *

Bailey woke early and logged onto the internet. He had a sequence of intricate levels of authentication and encryption in place. He didn't allow himself coffee before he performed them, because a single mistake would lock him out for twenty-four hours. A second mistake would destroy the machine, and the files. Nothing in his life was performed without precision, least of all the handling of his business.

Tim made him nervous. The parties had been effective, but it was never a good idea to dip too many times from the same well, and getting the right target into those parties was uncertain and rarely possible. And their homes were so close. Bailey was careful. Tim was flamboyant. Something was going to have to change.

He entered the last passcode and a simple message screen opened. He typed a lengthy address into a blank window, added a space, and typed the word "delivery." He closed the browser and turned off the computer. Nothing left but to fill time. Time also made him nervous; it was an opportunity for something to go wrong, and Bailey hated it when things went wrong.

His phone buzzed and he read the calendar notification. This was the day the HOA would inspect the lawn in the backyard. They would show up in about an hour and he had a few details to take care of. The garage door opened into the backyard. Unless you knew where to find the hidden door, and the stairs, that was all you would ever see. There was a panel hidden in the wall beside that door. Behind it were both fingerprint and retinal scanners. If you were not Bailey, or didn't have some serious tools, you weren't getting past the security. There was absolutely no indication that anything else was going on, but it never hurt to be careful. If anyone saw him circling the perfect lawn, they'd believe he was nervous and making sure things were perfect. They would be right, but they would also be dead wrong, because he had absolutely no worries with the grass, the shrubs, the height of his privacy fence or any other item that might concern his neighbors.

He had memorized the rules. More than once he'd mentioned to Tim that it would be a good idea to try a little harder to blend in. There were three neighbors who were either independently wealthy enough not to work or had home offices. They were always watching.

The fact that none of the others on the street varied from the HOA rules was good intel. Necessary intel. It meant someone was watching, and that someone would report violations. They would not be reporting Bailey, but he knew he was going to have to cut loose from Tim soon. That meant Tim would leave, or he would have to be handled. Bailey was not looking forward to a rebuild, or new surroundings. He intended to be around for a long time to come.

Before he checked on the garage and the yard, he brewed a pot of tea, adding sugar carefully, remembering his mentor's instructions. If a thing could be done, or done right, it could also be perfect. He intended to have a tall, chilled pitcher of sweet tea waiting for the HOA members. Details mattered.

* * *

Tim sipped coffee and watched the HOA approach Bailey's driveway in a solemn line. Led by Sam Burnett, they marched in lockstep. Eleanor Brothers with her perfectly coiffed gray beehive of gray hair and sensible shoes, Ed Leery, a ballcap tilted down over his eyes, dressed for work in jeans and polished boots. Tim thought the man was some sort of foreman but had only half paid attention when they met. The group was trailed by their final official member, Gina Daniels, who always looked sort of confused, but was stunning in a knee-length skirt and heels. Tim knew the type. She was probably a realtor, or a lawyer, counting on her looks to confuse the men she worked with into believing she was stupid.

Tim didn't watch because he cared about the HOA. He watched because he'd never been invited to Bailey's place, and there was a lot at stake. He also watched because too much of his well-being depended on the caution of a man he barely knew. A wrapper from a bag of chips rolled down his driveway. He ignored it as it flittered into the street and rolled along, almost as if it were following the group.

Sam Burnett turned, apparently hearing the rustle of the bag on the road. When he saw it, he glanced up, and Tim was nearly certain the man stared straight into his eyes. Tim continued sipping coffee. Who cared if a bit of trash blew down the street? There were more important things than making the neighbors happy. He hoped that Bailey understood that as well as he did, and that nothing would be out of place.

Tim had no more involvement in the previous night's transaction. He had no idea where the product would be delivered, to whom, or even if he'd over or underpriced his own part in it. It didn't matter. He needed to get ready for the next deal, and parties like his were an art form.

He headed for his office. He could check in with Bailey later. They'd never exchanged more than a few words, but maybe a beer, somewhere far from the neighborhood. Maybe not. Whatever came of the HOA inspection, they were going to have to communicate. It wasn't optimal. The less they knew about one another, the better. He kind of wished he didn't even know Bailey's name.

* * *

Bailey ushered the HOA members into his home and offered them tea. Sam declined, but Eleanor, Ed, and Gina accepted with emotionless smiles. The sense of going through a set of scripted motions hung heavy in the air, and Bailey's confidence began to slip. He gave them all a short tour of the home, a place they'd last seen when it had been trashed by the previous owner. Everything was in its place. The floors shone. There was no clutter. He'd left the back curtains and blinds open, so a hint of the lush green lawn was visible.

"Shall we get to it then?" Sam asked. He hadn't smiled, but he also hadn't frowned. He held a clipboard, and he kept checking his phone, except to Bailey it didn't look like any phone he'd ever seen.

"Of course. Follow me."

He led them down a short set of stairs to the garage. His car was parked, carefully centered, leaving plenty of room to reach the door to the backyard. He opened the door and held it, gesturing for the others to pass through. He noticed that, as he crossed the threshold, Sam glanced at the device in his hand. Definitely not a phone. Hairs stood up on Bailey's neck. Something was off, and he knew he had to get a handle on it quickly. He followed the others through the door and closed it behind them.

The fence had been painted. He'd placed a round table with four chairs near a fire pit that was complete with a spit for roasting meat. He saw Eleanor frowning at it and stepped forward.

"Only for neighborhood get-togethers," he said, offering a version of Sam's emotionless smile. "I thought it added to the aesthetic, but I don't entertain much. At all."

Sam's lip curled up at the corner. This time it was almost a smile. It fell short, but it gave Bailey hope. Then Sam glanced at the device a final time, clicked a button, and dropped it into his pocket.

"The yard looks good, Bailey," he said. "Everything looks good, really. I think we've seen enough, but..."

Here it comes, Bailey thought. He mentally ran through the places he'd cached weapons, inventoried his various "go" bags and calculated the sprint it would take to vault over the fence.

"Here's the thing," Sam continued. "You have met all the tenets of the HOA, and you have done so with precision and care. It's time you saw something we rarely show to anyone who is not a member of the council. Something... important."

Bailey stood very still, waiting.

Sam crossed the yard until they stood very close. He was aware of Clara's microphones.

"You need to take us to that quiet place," he said. "I'm not going to entertain arguments on its existence. We have things to discuss, and they are very private.

Do not worry about the young man. I do not care. None of us do."

Bailey met the older man's gaze, glanced around at the others, who appeared to be paying absolutely no attention, then nodded. His mind raced, but every scenario ended the same way. Either they would go below, talk, and things would change for the better, or they would go below and he'd do his best to end them all, lock them in the rest of the cells, seal the place, and move on.

With a smile that held absolutely no emotion, he waved his hand toward the garage door and the others followed him through, and in. Once they were inside, surprisingly, they turned their backs and stood very still, waiting. Even Sam. With a shrug, Bailey slid a finger into a small depression in the drywall. A scanner read his print, and a panel opened. He stepped closer, leaned in, and waited for the retinal scan to complete. The mechanism was silent. When the shift was complete, Bailey cleared his throat, and the others turned. Sam glanced at the doorway, raised an eyebrow. Again, just for a second, he nearly smiled.

Bailey led the way down the stairs. He had weapons stashed below, and other safety features, but he did not sense a threat, and until he did, he didn't intend to become one. The others piled in behind him, Sam Burnett bringing up the rear. When they were all inside, he flipped the switch that returned the garage door to its normal state. For better or worse, they were secure.

"Impressive," Sam said, taking a quick turn around the room. He glanced into the cell where the young man sat dejectedly, leaning back against the wall. Sam waved his hand, but the boy didn't see him. Sam pulled out the device from his pocket and laid it on the table.

"Very sensitive," he said. "Serves many purposes, one of them being a metal detector. Another is an electromagnetic field meter (emf) meter. We run serious background checks on those we hope will stay long-term. You've spent a lot at construction sites and home improvement stores, but even more at some pretty expensive tech sites. I could show you the files, but I'm sure you have copies."

"What do you want?" Bailey asked.

"We want what you want," Sam said. "Rules and borders. We have a much stricter HOA policy that is not shared with the general public. Your friend Tim, for instance, will never see it. He's becoming a problem."

"I know."

"There are solutions for every problem," Sam said. "Let's get down to this, shall we? I have things to attend to, as do we all. None of them are, of course, any of your business any more than whoever that is would be mine. We just need to go over the rules."

* * *

The first car was pulling up to Tim's house when the power went out. Dead. The entire block blacked out, the music stopped, and the couple in the car, twenty-something and already half-stoned, sat quietly in their seats, not bothering to open their doors. Tim, already pretending to sip a goblet of wine, stopped still in his doorway. He'd been about to greet the newcomers, but the silence was so sudden and complete, he couldn't bring himself to shatter it, even by stepping outside. Instead, he waited.

The electricity had been solid since he'd moved to the neighborhood, but he hadn't been there long. Most places he'd lived, power would go out in bad storms, or high winds, or when some idiot crashed a 4x4 truck into the wrong pole and took out a transformer. Then there had been noise and sparks. This felt different. It was if all life had been sucked from the entire block.

He saw no candles flickering in the windows. No one wandered out to the sidewalk with a flashlight. The couple in the car slowly backed out of the drive-way. The woman in the passenger seat gave him a small wave, and they rolled slowly back down the street. Their headlights painted long, eerie shadows on the homes and sidewalks, and then they were gone, and everything was totally dark.

Tim slowly backed in through the door and closed it behind him. He rarely locked it, but this time, he did. Something felt off, something a lot more serious than a power outage and a ruined party. He turned and headed back to the kitchen, setting his glass on the counter. He opened the refrigerator. He needed something to drink, but not alcohol. He had bottles of sparkling water on the bottom shelf, easy to find, even without the light.

He reached in, but stopped when his fingers came across something unexpected. Paper? He grabbed whatever it was and pulled out his phone. By the screen's light he saw he was holding an empty potato chip bag. He stared. He knew it had to be the same one that had blown down the street, but why was it here? How had it gotten inside his house and into the refrigerator? And why?

He glanced at the back door. The one Bailey used. He thought back quickly, tried to think if he'd slipped up, if he'd compromised the other man in some way, but his memory was nearly perfect, and he knew he'd handled it cleanly. Bailey was a pro. Who, then and why?

He crossed the kitchen and locked the back door. His gun was in his bedroom, and there were several rooms along the hall before he could reach it. Taking a cue from the slasher movies he'd enjoyed in college, he snagged the biggest knife from the block case on the counter and slipped into the hallway, listening carefully, and watching for darker shadows. He held the knife ready, but close to his chest and concealed by his forearm. He'd be ready for a surprise, but also set to attack. There had been tight situations before, but the darkness made him nervous. More accurately, what bothered him was the effort and reach it would take to create that darkness if it wasn't a naturally occurring outage. There were monitors, gauges, alarms of all sorts that regulated city power. An irregularity of this size, if someone had caused it on purpose, would require some serious connections and a lot of technical ability. And it was so quiet.

Surely neighbors were on the phones and calling it in. He only needed to avoid whoever had entered his house and wait them out. They were quiet. Or, more likely they'd sneaked in while he was out front, dropped off the wrapper as some weird neighborly warning, and hightailed it back into the darkness.

The first room he passed was the bathroom. He knew the door would be open; it was always open unless someone was inside. Party rules. What goes in always comes back out, and he didn't want that happening in his yard. For that matter, neither did the HOA. He took a breath, held the knife out, arms bent to thrust, and side-stepped the open doorway. Nothing.

He turned his back to the wall and inched toward the second door, a spare bedroom he'd converted to his office. That door would be closed and locked. It was never accessible unless he was the only one in the house. He kept his back to that wall. There was a second bedroom across from it, a sort of guest bedroom lounge with a TV, a pull-out sofa, chairs, and a table. There were a lot of places to hide inside, but there was only one way in, or out. He didn't hesitate, he leaped past the door, knife at the ready, landed on the far side and ran for his bedroom at the end of the hall. He stopped at the door. It was open. It should not have been.

He held his breath and flattened against the wall. If someone was inside, they might already have located the gun. They might be between him and the nightstand where it was stored. They could be almost anywhere. He held his breath and listened. There was nothing. No breathing, no shifting of feet. Very slowly, he eased around the doorframe into the room. Forcing his heartbeat to remain steady, he closed his eyes, hoping to acclimate his eyes to the dark. He moved along the wall to his right toward the nightstand. As he went, he turned slowly from side to side, the knife ready. He saw nothing but vague shadows. Every few steps he stopped and listened, but there was still nothing.

He took a long, slow breath, and crossed the room. He had one hand out, reaching for the nightstand, the other holding the knife, but he made the transit safely. He pulled open the drawer, reached inside, and grabbed the .45 with a sigh of relief. He dropped the knife, raised the gun, and scanned the room.

The lights flickered once, twice, and then flashed to life. Tim blinked, trying to steady his gaze. When it all settled, he saw Sam from the HOA standing across from him. He held a clipboard, and he seemed to be reading something.

"What the FUCK are you doing in my house?" Tim asked, waving the .45 from side to side. "What's going on, Sam? Did you kill the power?"

Sam glanced up.

"I think I'll be asking the questions," he said. "You've violated," he glanced back to the clipboard, "no fewer than ten HOA rules in the last week."

Tim blinked.

"Are you kidding me? You killed power to the entire neighborhood, broke into my house, stuffed trash in my refrigerator and hid in my bedroom because I played my music too late, and violated your trash rules?"

"All of those reasons would be sufficient," Sam said, looking back up from the clipboard. "But that's not why I'm here. I'm here because you have been indiscreet. You don't appear to even have read the rules, let alone followed them. Rules, and the words that make them up, matter. You aren't the only person in the neighborhood with secrets. You are probably the only one, however, who doesn't know that others are aware of yours. We know about the parties, the abductions, the payoffs. We know you are associated with another HOA member, and that you have been far too careless in your dealings. To be blunt, Mr. Johnson, we don't believe you are the right sort of neighbor. We require a certain discretion. That should have been obvious in the HOA."

Tim lowered the gun and stared. "You're fucking crazy," he said. "I'll give you exactly a minute to get out of my house before I shoot you, call the police, and report you for breaking and entering. Not sure I won't do that anyway once you're gone."

There was a sound to his left, and Tim spun. Bailey stood in the doorway, watching him with a steady gaze. Tim didn't hesitate. He lifted the gun and pulled the trigger. Once. Twice, a dozen times. Nothing happened, but he couldn't stop his finger from tightening again, and again as panic grew. He turned at a sound behind him, too late, as someone stepped from his closet and pressed a damp cloth across his nose and mouth. He tried to struggle, he swung his elbow back, but hit nothing. Then, everything went dark.

* * *

Tim shook his head groggily and forced his eyes open. The light was dim. He was lying on a narrow cot. There was a sink, a table, and a chair. There was some sort of camper-style toilet in the corner.

What the fuck? he thought.

He sat up. The wall in front of him appeared to be glass, but he couldn't see a thing through it. As he stood, the light brightened. He still couldn't see through the glass. He turned and noticed there were papers stacked on the table. His thoughts were still muddy, but he made his way to the chair, sat, and flipped through them.

There were three separate documents. The first was a typed note. The second was a copy of the HOA he'd signed when he moved into the neighborhood, but thicker. The third appeared to be a receipt, or some sort of bill of sale. He started with the note. It

was short and to the point. He glanced down and saw
that it was signed by Clara, the woman across the
street.

Tim,

*It is too late to explain to you how much words matter.
You read and signed the HOA agreement, but apparently
did not realize the rules contained in that document
weren't suggestions. You have been noisy, intrusive, rude,
and dismissive. We would have revoked your acceptance
and forced you to move.*

*Of course, we all know these were not your only viola-
tions. If you had managed to follow the few simple rules, as
all of us have done, you might have received the extended
HOA (enclosed) and understood your actions were reckless.
Drawing attention to the neighborhood is the most egre-
gious violation possible. Young, rich men and women are
all missing after attending parties at a single location.
There has been no connection made to date. Justin Barnes,
two houses down from you on the left, works for the
Attorney General's office. He has watched the cases carefully. Alternate statements have surfaced, created by
Bailey's connections. The waters have muddied, and when
they come looking for you, records will show you have
moved overseas. Airline records will show you boarding in
New York and departing in Amsterdam. The details will
not matter.*

*Suffice it to say, there is no one in this neighborhood
without secrets. We know everything there is to know about
all members of the HOA. It's available for a price, much of
it for free, and you aren't particularly careful. You can*

peruse the extended HOA at your leisure if you wish. There is no point. The last document will explain.

I am sorry things didn't work out.

Tim fumbled with the cover of the HOA, and then pushed it aside. He grabbed the receipt and scanned the details.

Procured: the man responsible for your son's disappearance:

Terms: Payment prior to delivery.

Total Payment: Delivery of product with DNA evidence of missing boy.

Provide delivery details within twenty-four hours.

Provide DNA Evidence upon delivery.

Tim stared. Who could this have been sent to? He flipped back through his memories. He counted at least three names, just since he'd moved to the neighborhood. It wouldn't be one of those. It would be somewhere else, some other home he'd left behind. Some other connection he'd had before Bailey. None of Bailey's targets had been related to any ransom. In fact, none of them had ever made any sense, but the payments had been quick, and the procurements had been handled efficiently. This note had to be from someone with money and connections.

That meant it was a job he'd completed before meeting Bailey. Before moving to this neighborhood. How could they have information like that? How could they provide DNA evidence that should be long gone, and who had it been? Who were they planning on delivering him to?

He turned toward the window, suddenly certain they were all there, the entire HOA, watching him through that window. He stood and walked to the glass, staring out. Behind him, on the wall, a hissing sound rose. The room filled quickly with gas, and his eyesight blurred. *They were watching,* he thought. *All of them. All along. Someone is always watching...*

He didn't feel his head hit the table, or his body slump in the chair. The world, and the words, faded to shadow.

END

CHAPTER TWO

Andrea typed that final word and sat back, bewildered. Her mouth was dry. Her fingers were cramped and her back felt as if she'd been bent into a pretzel. She clicked "save," pushed away from the desk, and stood shakily.

She'd stood too quickly. She staggered and nearly fell as she backpedaled. Only the wall prevented a nasty fall. Pressing both palms against it, she righted herself and glanced around the room. On the wall hung the kitschy clock she and Jen had bought at a writer's convention, it's three-dimensional gears turning and interlocking. She stared at the hands. Six o'clock. How was that possible? She'd only sat down to write a little before midnight. She couldn't remember using the restroom or getting a drink. Her legs shook.

She stumbled out of the room, taking deep breaths and trying to focus her thoughts. She caught the scent of coffee and headed for the kitchen. As she passed the family room, she saw the sun had risen, and heard cars passing on the street. A horn blared. None of it felt real. She stopped in the doorway to the kitchen.

Jen was breaking eggs over a frying pan. The coffee had finished brewing and was poured into the chrome carafe they used to keep it hot and fresh. Everything about the morning was the same as any other except, how was it morning? Where had the night gone? What had she written?

She recalled the words, vaguely. She still had images floating in her head that she knew were embedded in the story, but she couldn't concentrate enough to draw them together.

Jen glanced up and frowned, then went back to work on the eggs and bacon. "You were certainly focused," she said, flipping one of the eggs. "I came in to check on you a dozen times. I couldn't even get you to look away from the screen."

As the eggs sizzled, Andrea took a deep breath and stepped into the room. "I'm sorry. I don't know what came over me. I've never written like that or that much in one sitting, even with a deadline. I . . ."

She stopped talking and crossed to the coffee maker. She poured a cup and held it under her nose, inhaling the aroma. "I'm sorry," she repeated.

Jen grabbed two plates, loaded them up and carried them to the table. She shook her head and smiled.

"Sit down and eat. Then we'll put you into a shower and then bed. There's nothing important happening today, and you have to get some sleep. I can't say I'm a fan of manic writing episodes, but I've never seen you so focused. I can't wait to read it. I assume it's not about Teresa Vincent."

Andrea sat gratefully, put her mug on the table, and reached for a fork. Now that the food was in front of her, she realized she was starving. She couldn't remember ever being so hungry and was thinking about adding toast with butter and jam.

"I haven't processed it yet," she said. "I mean, I know what I wrote for the most part, but I have no clear memory of the actual writing. I was on a website, and there was a writing prompt. It triggered something. Something I didn't know I was holding back. And I don't think it's the end. More like some kind of strange new beginning. I honestly can't imagine sitting down to type "Teresa Vincent" in any context. It's a little frightening."

"A writing prompt? Like what, a photograph? A piece of a poem you're supposed to be inspired by? That feels a little derivative."

Andrea shook her head. "Nothing like that. I don't even really remember how I got there. I remember you mentioning people using prompts to break through writer's block and I just searched for it. It's almost too cliché – 'mywritingprompts.com.'"

"Sounds interesting. Whatever it was, it set you off. You remember what we talked about," Jen said. "You don't have to waste your life writing things you don't want to. If you want, I'll talk to Sylvia. She's more than a good agent, she has connections. She's mentioned that she has connections with some seriously talented, hungry young ghostwriters. First you let them write a couple things with both of your names on the covers, then you hand over the series and rake in the royalties, and, in the meantime, you see where this new muse leads. Or. . . I can handle that. . .”

Andrea nodded, but Jen's words didn't sink in fully. “I want that,” she said, “but I want more. Whatever that is in there, whatever I do next? I don't want anyone to know it's me. I want to start over, prove myself, find a new world of readers.” She laughed nervously. “I sound crazy. I have no idea what I want, but I know I want toast, and jam, another cup of coffee, and my bed. I feel like I've been up for three days on a bender.”

“You've got it,” Jen said, rising. “Finish that up, I'll make the toast. Maybe I'll join you in that shower.”

Andrea smiled, and this time it felt real, and deep. She sat and ate. She drank the coffee and a second cup. Then, after hugging Jen tightly, she headed off to shower and sleep. The strange spell the story she'd written had cast was fading, and all she felt was exhaustion deeper than anything she could remember.

* * *

There was no scent of coffee when Andrea awoke late that evening. Most of the lights in the house were off, and there was no sound. No low whisper of television voices muted so she wouldn't be disturbed. No soft music floating out from the family room speakers. Nothing.

She sat up, held her head in her hands for a long moment, then slipped off the bed and grabbed the terrycloth robe off the chair. As she moved into the hall she flipped on the lights.

"Jen?" she said. Then, louder, "Jen, are you awake?"

She got no response, but there was light in the kitchen, so she headed that way quietly. Something felt off. Jen was always considerate, solicitous to a fault, but this was next level. No lights after sunset? No sound?

When she reached the doorway to the kitchen, Andrea stopped and stared. Jen was seated on one of the stools at the breakfast bar. All across the surface she'd spread papers, lined up in rows. The lamp from the desk in the living room had been placed on the corner of the Formica surface, lighting the scattered pages in a pool of brilliance.

Jen was bent over, staring at one of the pages intently. Andrea cleared her throat. At first, she didn't even get a reaction. She stepped into the kitchen, and Jen glanced up. Her eyes were wide and haunted. She didn't even seem to know who she was looking at.

"Jen," Andrea repeated, "What are you doing? What *is* that?"

Jen stared a moment longer, then turned back as if

noticing all the papers spread out before her for the first time. She shook her head, as if confused, then turned back to Andrea.

"I'm going through the HOA agreement," she said. "I never really read it when we moved in, just signed, and smiled and nodded. There are so many rules. . ."

Tumblers rolled and clicked in Andrea's mind. She had not thought about the story since falling asleep, and there had been no dreams.

"You read the story," she said softly.

Jen smiled nervously. "You left the screen open. I saved it to be sure you had it, and once I'd started, I couldn't stop. But now? I can't seem to get it out of my head. I mean, what if we aren't handling our garbage properly? Is our fence the right height? I've never checked. I don't know how close our flower beds are to the easement. Do you? How many of our neighbors do you know?"

Andrea could only stare. She glanced at the documents spread across the tabletop and then back at Jen. "You," she said. "Me. We are getting a bottle of wine, and you are decompressing. Are you kidding me? We are breaking no rules."

"There are so many words," Jen said.

"We have been approved. They come once a month to assess things. We are fine. Our neighbors are not hiding bodies beneath swimming pools. In fact, swimming pools are allowed. I *did* read the HOA. You know me. The words. They always matter."

Jen's head jerked and she locked onto Andrea's gaze. "They do. They really do. I never. . ."

Andrea put an arm around Jen's shoulder and helped her to her feet. She led her out of the room. The HOA was forgotten. The pool of light from the lamp splashed across the words and the rules, but no one paid attention. Andrea got Jen onto the love seat in the living room, found a bottle of red wine and poured.

"Besides the craziness in there," Andrea said, nodding to the kitchen, "You liked it? It works? It's so different. . ."

"It's amazing," Jen said. She closed her eyes for a moment, sipped the wine, and then met Andrea's gaze. She seemed a little more focused. "I have no idea what came over me. I kept thinking about those people, how they seemed normal, and ordinary, and how wrong it all was. And right out in the open. It felt too real."

Andrea blinked. Just for a moment, she had the sensation of being watched, and glanced down the hall toward the front door. "I'm glad you liked it, but it's a story. That's all. I've never seen anyone get a violation notice here, not even the lady down the street with like a thousand gnomes in her front yard, or that guy with the junk car in his backyard."

"I know," Jen said. "I know. It's just. . ."

"I need your help with something," Andrea said. "I need you to make me a website."

"You already have an *amazing* website. I mean, Jesus, you have what, 1.5 million followers on social media and your blog blows up the internet every time you post?!"

"Exactly. I need a new site because I'm not planning on submitting this story, or any of those I'm working on, under my name. The idea is to see if people will find them, read them, and like them if they don't know the author. I can't even let there be a rumor it might be me."

"Okay. . . but if not you, who? Who wrote that story?"

Andrea barely hesitated. "Robin," she said. "Robin Orestad. I'll explain that to you later, but can you do it? Something very simple, but catchy enough it won't seem like someone's new hobby? Serious, but without much content. I guess there needs to be a blog. I'll write something about writing prompts, finally being ready to release some of my work. . . I've seen a million sites like that. Maybe we can anonymously put the link out a few places with simple comments about the story being interesting, and then we wait?"

"That could be a long wait," Jen said. "You know how this business is. Without some visibility, getting people to not only visit a new author's site, but to read a story that long, is a crapshoot.'"

"Then we'll have to roll those dice," Andrea said. "I can be working on the next thing in the meantime. That should distract me some."

"Okay, well, I can have something basic up, with your story, by tonight. I can work a little SEO magic and use a few of the anonymous accounts we have to pass the link. I can even create a script that drops it on social media sites with a nice, simple graphic, but no real info. Should I be looking up Robin Orestad on Facebook to make sure whoever that is, isn't going to sue?"

"It's a name from the past. I haven't had any contact with her since high school, but I did see a notice on the invitation to my tenth reunion. She got married, has a different name, something like Illian, I think, so I wouldn't worry about her catching on. She was very clearly not a fan of my work, even back then. In a way, none of this would have happened without her, but she has no idea."

"Consider it done," Jen said. "I need to get my mind off how far our garbage can is pulled back from the easement. Maybe this will help."

Andrea started to laugh but stopped herself. Something in the faraway expression on Jen's face prevented it. When she was alone again, she gathered the pages of the HOA Agreement and carried them back to her office. She had a locked drawer in her desk. Jen didn't have a key; there had never seemed a reason to get one made. It contained a small cashbox, some important contracts, and a very old bottle of scotch. She opened it, tucked the HOA contract back behind the scotch, locked it and pocketed the key. Whatever had happened while she was asleep, she felt better knowing Jen couldn't return to her new obsession.

That done, she powered up her computer. She'd been thinking, trying to come up with a new idea, a next *thing*, but her mind remained blank. She remembered the previous story, and the prompt, but the obsession that had gripped her before she began writing was missing. Surely it wasn't going to be one and done.

She opened her browser and clicked MyWritingPrompts.com. The screen flickered once, and then the familiar nearly blank screen appeared. The text read:

ASSIGNMENT COMPLETE. PRESS ENTER FOR NEXT
PROMPT.

She stared at it. There was no way whoever ran that site knew she'd completed her story. It had to be configured so that coming back was an indicator. But why would you come back if you failed or if the prompt didn't work? There was no reason to run a site that didn't provide anything new to its users. She tried to conjure an image of a tired old journalist, or an English professor, creating the prompts and running them past countless hopefuls. It could be an experiment, or a study of some sort. Maybe there was a goal at the end, some writers' group, or offer for publication. It didn't matter. The first prompt had worked, and she was hopeful that whatever came next would do the same. If not, she would be no worse off for the effort.

She pressed ENTER and waited.

The prompt appeared, just as before. This time, a single word. It remained for less than a minute, and then, just like before, the screen blanked and the familiar, though slightly different, words appeared.

YOU HAVE BEEN SUCCESSFULLY LOGGED OFF:
PROMPT VALID FOR TWENTY-FOUR HOURS.

Absently, Andrea grabbed a pencil and notepad. She copied down the word, then sat back, staring at the screen.

"Shunned."

A moment later, she leaned forward and began to type.

"SHUNNED"

From the time Jackson was a small child, he'd lived a dual existence. In one world, he was so alone it felt like the air he breathed had never been touched by another set of lungs, that the only dust in the air had sloughed from his dying skin. It was like no set of eyes had ever seen or noticed him, no voice had reached him or reached out to him, because describing himself as insignificant would have implied the possibility of a significance that never existed.

His other life was layered in the expectations and disappointments of others, in failures to comply and the inability to change. His parents were members of the Church of New Light, a congregation so strict, Sundays felt like a walk into the past with walls closing in on all sides, compressing his heart and squashing his soul. He'd believed in that soul in the early days. He wanted to believe in salvation, but knew he wasn't worthy. He sang, and he prayed, and it echoed through the shadows of his mind. He memorized the words, the rituals, answered with the proper words when spoken to and never spoke first. But that belief they all espoused, the faraway dead-certain glint in their eyes, evaded him. In fact, it mocked him, tattooing his arms with colored swaths of sunlight cutting through stained-glass saints and bleeding saviors who touched him no more deeply than the passing wings of a fly.

The worst thing was that his parents knew. The others? He couldn't tell. He knew his mother and father wouldn't speak of it. He was their shame in private and their shining beacon in public. He always knew the right things to say, dressed to perfection, answered politely, and volunteered tirelessly. He had no friends, but then, he also had no enemies because he was simply there. Like the pews and the hymnals, the baptismal pool, and the altar.

If he was in church, he worked, and they worked with him. If he wasn't there, no one noticed. He doubted Pastor Grimes even asked his parents why their son wasn't in attendance on days he was ill or visiting his grandparents.

That world was the one where he felt most trapped. With so many rules, temptations he was forbidden to notice, and secrets that could never be shared, even if there'd been anyone to share them with. It was hard to breathe. He saw through the masks and lies of others. He saw their gazes linger where they shouldn't, overheard them talking in hushed voices, and he wondered how, despite that, they felt the cleaning light the pastor preached about, shared their belief in a greater power that would lead them to a place of salvation. It felt as if, no matter his efforts, the universe, any deity that might actually exist, even the world, and life, had shunned him from birth. Shunning was a word that had stuck with him, one that he'd studied and rolled over his tongue.

He'd heard the sermons. Shunning was for those who broke the commandments. It was for the sexually promiscuous, the idol worshippers, the drunkards, and criminals. Jackson was none of those things, at least not outwardly, and he'd tried everything to prevent their invasion of his internal world. He had desires. He saw and heard things that intrigued him, but he tucked them away. He buried them and studied more. He smiled, nodded, and wondered why his mother watched him with such disapproval.

It was inevitable that the two worlds would inter-sect. The one thing that would not let go of him was the shunning. It wasn't a thing that could be passive. It could not redeem him if it only happened in his mind. Glen Tambour, who directed the choir, was sleeping with the second tenor, Rose Glover, on the side. They claimed it was private voice lessons, but Jackson had passed by the doors of Tambour's office and heard their voices, and there had been no harmony. Neither of them was shunned, so clearly what they were doing was either acceptable, or simply not sinful enough to warrant notice.

Jackson's father kept a bottle of whiskey in the garage, where he'd been working on restoring a vintage Ford coupe with little progress for going on fifteen years. His mother never entered that space. Jackson wasn't certain if she knew and was unwilling to walk in and confirm his transgression, or if she was too busy with her hidden pack of cigarettes and the small bottle of Xanax she kept in her vanity.

The one thing Jackson was certain of, was that if he were to be shunned, he wanted it to be something he felt. He wanted it to be something he earned. He had always believed it was his lot in life, but the more he came to understand the word, the less certain he became that it felt right. If he simply didn't exist to the rest of the world as more than a token disappointment to his parents, what did it mean? What did it matter? He couldn't be shunned until he'd been noticed, and he'd done absolutely nothing in eighteen years of life to be noticed. He wasn't shunned, he was forgotten.

* * *

"Brothers and sisters, as we read in Second Thessalonians 3:14-15, 'If anyone does not obey what we say in this letter, take note of that person, and have nothing to do with him, that he may be ashamed. Do not regard him as an enemy but warn him as a brother."

Jackson sat stock-still, listening. He glanced at his father on his right. Nothing could have distracted the man from the words he was hearing, certainly not the gaze of his only child. Beyond his father, Jackson's mother leaned forward, her hands clutched to her breast as if hearing some sort of angelic choir, instead of a red-faced, blustery old man who spit at the end of every sentence, punctuating the verses crafted into a message of hope and salvation with a spray of saliva that glittered in the brilliance of the spotlight shining down on him.

As a brother, Jackson thought. No one had treated him as a brother since he'd first entered the doors of the chapel. Nor had they explained what he'd done to deserve his complete anonymity. No hand reached into the void to pull him free, or even suggested that, as Christians, it was their duty.

Proverbs urged that the wicked be purged. That would be better. If they ostracized him, accused him of all the things he'd thought about doing, but never acted on, he would feel alive. If they tried to save him, to draw him into the fold, or the flock, or whatever Pastor Grimes was calling it this week, successfully or not, it would mean he existed. If one of the girls or boys his age would catch him staring, a thing he did constantly, and call him out on it, he would gladly accept whatever white-hot shame confession could bring. None of that ever happened.

Finally, one morning, one sabbath day, he decided to play the hand that was dealt him. The world would accept him, or reject him, but they *would* acknowledge him. He decided to start at home with his family and give them the first opportunity to make things right. It only seemed fair. They'd been the first to fail to see him.

Breakfast was a routine. His mother would either put out boxes of cereal and a gallon of milk, or cook eggs, toast, and bacon. She always served him his fair share. She always cleaned the dishes he dutifully carried to the kitchen. She never asked if he wanted anything different, or how he liked the eggs. Those were pleasantries reserved for his father.

This morning, it was cereal. Jackson stared at the bowl, the glass of orange juice beside it, the carton of milk and the three boxes of various healthy choices. His father was reading a paper copy of the morning paper, a thing that, despite the world moving on rapidly, he did religiously. That was a word that had lost its shine for Jackson, but it seemed appropriate. As he read, his father would grunt, sigh, laugh, or rattle the pages in anger. He never shared the source of any of those emotions, particularly not with Jackson. His mother had almost as little interest in the news as she did in her son.

Jackson reached out, opened a box of cereal, and poured. He filled the bowl to the rim, and then, a bit more. It mounded on top, and he used his spoon to press it back in around the edges. No one noticed. He opened the milk and poured it in a slow trickle, letting it work through the flakes. He stopped pouring and capped the milk just as they rose like a slow eruption.

He worked the spoon down past the level of the milk and slid the bowl closer.

His father's paper rustled. His mother was at the stove, frying bacon and eggs that would not be offered. He heard the sizzle of the grease. The scrape of the cast-iron pan on the burner of the old gas stove. He heard his father chuckle and turn to the next page of the news.

Jackson drew back his arm, closed his eyes, thinking he really ought to say a prayer, or ask for some sort of forgiveness. Then he swung his hand in a quick arc, palm open, and drove the over-filled bowl off the table. It flew across the room and struck the wall. The bowl shattered and Jackson watched, fascinated, as the milk splashed in all directions. The world seemed to have slowed, and he saw the patterns spreading in the air, the flakes dripping milk. He saw droplets hit and soak into the pages of his father's paper.

Then he waited. His mother turned, frowned at the wall. She went to the pantry and came back with a bucket, mop, broom, and dustpan. His father glanced at his paper, confused, then shook his head, and returned to his reading. Jackson sat and watched as the mess was cleaned up around him. Then breakfast was served to his father, and the rest of the dishes were cleared away. His parents rose and left the room. A few seconds later, Jackson followed, heading to his room to dress for church.

* * *

Jackson sat quietly beside his mother as Pastor Grimes read passages from the Bible, punctuating them with exhortations to be pure, and to seek the truth. Truth was a word that eluded Jackson. He'd stared into the eyes of too many who followed what they believed was truth or that they were speaking it. He thought this knowledge in itself was his own truth, and that it was another cruel trick. Others could share their myriad truths, argue about them, laugh when they were ludicrous, or impossible. Jackson could have stood where Pastor Grimes stood, microphone in hand, and shared what he believed, and no one would hear him. They might not leave. They might watch him, and listen, but when he was finished and left that altar, it would be like the moment when a paused video resumed. Their lives would continue, and no one would remember.

Pastor Grimes assured them that there was one way, and one truth. Jackson wasn't certain if the man was just repeating ancient lies, or if he truly believed it. If he did, it was strange that he clearly didn't adhere to that one truth – at least not the one in scripture. No one did, but for some reason among all the hugs and "brother this," and "sister that" they seemed to think they did. Or that it didn't matter, if others believed they did.

The choir raised their voices and sang. Pastor Grimes began the call to baptism. Every Sunday the result was the same. A man, or a woman would stand. They would stumble down the aisle and make their way to the front. One here, one there, the faithful lurching to their feet and falling over themselves to reach the altar.

At the same time, the ushers would make their way to the front, and, amid Hallelujahs and Praise the Lords, they would begin passing the heavy copper plates, lined in velvet to maintain the holy silence, gathering the money to keep the stained-glass windows clean and the communion wine flowing. The money that fueled Pastor Grimes' late model Mercedes.

Jackson rose. His mother glanced at him, as if confused, then turned back to Grimes. Silently, those seated between Jackson and the aisle drew in their legs and let him pass. There were no smiles of encouragement, or stares. He made it to the main aisle and hurried forward. Several others had risen, but he intended to reach the altar first. Pastor Grimes stared at him. His words fumbled, just for a moment, then he took Jackson by the arm and led him up and back, through a curtained alcove behind the baptismal pool.

The lights were bright. Below him, Jackson saw the others, lining up, waiting their turn. One of the ushers had stationed himself at the head of that line. He would escort them back, one after the other, until all sins were cleansed, and the collection plates over-flowed. Near the middle of the line, just for a second, Jackson caught the eye of a girl a little older than he was. She actually seemed to smile, but the moment passed.

Jackson had shed his shoes and socks. Pastor Grimes wore his robes, and whatever was beneath. They stepped into the pool and faced out to where Jackson knew his parents and the congregation watched. The lights blinded him. He turned to the pastor, who still seemed slightly confused, as if he didn't know why he was there, or he'd forgotten something important. Jackson pulled away from the older man and faced out into the void. He reached into the pocket of his pants and drew out the kitchen knife he'd snatched after breakfast. He'd purposefully grabbed the one that looked most like a slasher in a horror movie would carry, because he needed to break through the world's apathy, and he thought – maybe – the proper blade might catch their attention and focus their emotions.

Behind him, Pastor Grimes mumbled something, but he didn't step forward. Jackson gripped the handle of the knife, spun it toward himself and said, as loudly as he could, "Forgive me."

He plunged the blade into his throat. For just a moment he stood very still staring out into the gathered faithful. Waiting. There was heat, and his legs grew very suddenly weak. He heard Pastor Grimes climbing from the pool. Tears ran down Jackson's cheeks, but he stood, as long as he could, and then, very slowly, he sank into the pool, his blood spreading into the clear, pristine water. As his eyes neared the surface, he saw a reflection. Very clearly, with no obstruction, he saw Pastor Grimes, staring past him. Through him. Then all was darkness.

* * *

The usher brought the first of the faithful up through the curtains. Pastor Grimes shook his head, then smiled. He glanced into the pool. The water was clear and glittering in the bright light. He frowned slightly. There was something floating on the pool, a bit of cloth? He reached down to grip it by the edge and pull it free, but his fingers touching the surface of the pool dispersed it, or broke the mirage, and he stood.

A woman was coming up the stairs, tears streaming down her cheeks and ruining her makeup. He took her hand and stepped toward the pool, feeling, just for a second, that he'd forgotten something important. Off to one side, the choir reached the crescendo of a mighty amen, and Pastor Grimes stepped into the pool.

END

CHAPTER THREE

Andrea shook her head. The room was fuzzy, and her lips were so dry and parched she barely had the strength to part them. When she did, it hurt. She didn't look at the screen. She spun her chair, every movement highlighting a new stiffness or pain. She stood slowly, tried to orient herself, then staggered. She hit the wall hard enough that she bit her lip, and that pain brought her back to her senses.

She stood and leaned on the wall, breathing deeply. She wanted to close her eyes, but knew if she did, she would fall. A glance down the hallway showed her only one light was on, the nightlight in the kitchen. She righted herself and headed toward it.

Suddenly water was all she could think of. Her steps were uneven, and she had to use the wall for balance. She made it to the refrigerator without falling, pressed her hands together under the spout of the filtered water and dipped her head, drinking greedily and letting the cool liquid cascade over her fingers to the floor and down the front of her T-shirt. She gasped for breath, leaned in again and banged her head painfully on the metal frame of the ice dispenser. She drank again, turned, and leaned against the stainless steel door.

The nightlight was dim, and her eyes were dry and sticky. She had no idea how she could have been typing, and no idea what she'd typed. She had a memory of a boy, and a stairway, but it did not seem right. She had the vague notion she should return to the desk and save the file, but one glance down that hallway was enough to convince her she wouldn't make it. The living room was only a few feet away, with a couch and pillows. The bedroom was even farther and she didn't want to wake Jen.

She glanced at the fancy home security/shopping screen Jen had bought her for her birthday as she passed and stopped. The screen displayed recipes, news bytes, and in big digital characters, the time and date. The wrong date. A date a full day past the last time she'd checked, and it was nearly midnight.

She glanced back over her shoulder. Words flashed through her mind.

"PROMPT GOOD FOR TWENTY-FOUR HOURS"

She felt her knees starting to give, stumbled to the couch, and fell across it lengthwise. She pulled the afghan down over herself and tucked a pillow under her head. She was out before she could consider whether it was even possible she'd been typing for twenty-four hours. There weren't enough words. There weren't enough pages, but when clocks lie, it's usually because they stop, not because they jump hours into the future.

* * *

The scent of bacon, coffee, and toast brought Andrea slowly back to reality. She pulled the blanket off and sat up very slowly. Her head pounded and her mouth was dry. She headed to the hall bathroom first. The scent of breakfast and the thought of spewing it all over the table warred for just a second, but instinct won. She scrambled for the bathroom, closed the door behind herself and leaned heavily against it.

She stripped and turned on the shower. While the water warmed, she fought back the urge to vomit and sat on the toilet. She felt like she had to void every ounce of moisture in her body, and at the same time if she'd had a pitcher of water, she'd chug it until she choked. Her head pounded and her eyes burned.

When she felt strong and empty enough to rise, she slipped into the shower. The water was hot, but not too hot. She let it splash over her face, then turned, and felt it softly massage the back of her neck. She washed slowly, careful not to slip, and forced her mind to regain its focus.

She toweled dry, glanced at the clothes she'd been wearing for – how long? She left them on the floor and, though the coffee and bacon screamed at her to stop, she made her way down the hall to the bedroom. A few moments later she emerged in a pair of clean sweats, her damp hair tied back, and her steps a little steadier.

There was no sign of Jen in the kitchen. A place had been set for her. The coffee pot had been turned off and cleaned. She saw the insulated carafe beside a plate of eggs, bacon, and toast. She looked down the hall, frowned, but couldn't resist the bacon any longer. She poured a cup of the coffee and attacked the food. It was gone far too soon, and then she gulped the coffee. She poured a second cup and popped two more slices of bread into the toaster. She grabbed a jar of marmalade from the fridge and stood, tapping her foot as the toaster heated.

The story was coming back to her in bits, and, again, she worried that she had not saved it, that there could have been a power loss, or some weird computer glitch. And there were pieces that she remembered, but did not believe she'd written. Some of them felt too real, too personal. When the toast was ready, she hurried back to her den.

The monitor was blank, and her heart sank. Then, she saw the neatly stacked paper beside the keyboard. She scanned quickly through the first page. It was the story. There was no title, but all of it was there. She tapped the mouse, and her login screen appeared. She dropped into her chair and entered her password.

The browser was open, displaying the page Jen had made for her. Or, the page Jen had made for Robin Orestad. There was a short post about finally putting the work out there, hoping someone would read. There was also a link to the story.

Andrea followed that link, scrolled quickly through the perfectly formatted words, then couldn't stand it any longer. She scrolled to the bottom. There was a single comment, from Robin Orestad herself.

"I hope some of you will like it. I'm leaving this comment so the story won't sit here with none. Paranoid, I know, but there it is. -R.O."

There were more comments. A lot more comments. She tried to read them, thought about responding, but they were strange. . . most seemed to be about home-owners' associations and spy cameras, and something called the Deep State. Some felt almost frantic. She remembered how Jen had reacted, thought about the HOA locked in her file cabinet, and shook her head.

Andrea closed the browser and opened her e-mail. She had a query from her agent about her next book. There was the usual spam, a few notes from fans and friends. She scrolled down the account tree on the left side of the program until she reached the account they'd created for Robin. They had not published it publicly on the site to avoid the flood, but a few people had found it, it seemed. Andrea opened the first:

• • •

Dear Robin,

I have read your story and I have to say, I will never look at my neighbors in the same way. You have a power to your words that I find compelling and even addictive. I've read the story more than once.

I publish a literary magazine online, The Edge, *where I try to showcase new voices that I believe will shape the world of fiction for years to come. (I know, lofty goals for a small start-up publication). This may be forward of me, but I am wondering if you have other stories, and, if you do, if you might be interested in submitting one of them to* The Edge? *We only pay a small honorarium, twenty five dollars per story, and I'm not naïve enough to try and tell you that the exposure is worth your work. I just figured that not asking would be worse than asking and getting a no. I hope to hear from you soon.*

Melinda Ross

Editor, The Edge

There was a link, and Andrea clicked it. *The Edge* was a well-designed internet periodical. There were sections for reviews, essays, fiction, poetry, and a clever "About" page describing the editor's vision. There were thousands of "webzines" available, but most of them were either closed for submissions, narrow in focus, or simply run by editors and publishers who lacked the experience to choose quality stories, or to turn away their friends.

There was something a little too familiar in the

layout, as if maybe it had been copied from something bigger, or she'd seen one very similar in the past, but she couldn't place it.

There were three stories featured currently. Andrea read through them quickly. The first was a narrative from the perspective of a young black man. It highlighted the fears, and realities the author had experienced in society, and drove through pain to a very dark, but satisfying, ending.

The others were equally well-written, and a few more clicks showed her that the authors were making waves of their own, on the brink of discovery.

She opened the file for her new story. She had not given it a title, but the decision was simple. She remembered the prompt. She typed SHUNNED, centered it, and added Robin Orestad's name.

Without reading through the manuscript, or checking the website for word limits, or formatting guidelines, Andrea opened a reply to the e-mail she'd received, and attached the story. She kept her note short.

Melinda,

Many thanks for your kind words about my work. I have only just begun this writing journey, and I've no idea where it's going to take me. I have read the current issue of your webzine, and the stories are top-notch, particularly the one by the young African American author.

I have only one story available, and I hope it's not too

*long, and that it suits your needs. I will eagerly await your
decision,*

    Robin Orestad

After attaching and sending the story, Andrea
skimmed the rest of the e-mail, both hers, and that of
the new Robin account. Nothing caught her eye, so she
shut down, and went in search of Jen. She needed to
decompress, and to apologize for whatever it was that
had kept her glued to that keyboard for so long. She
knew she was being selfish, even if she didn't know
how it had happened, or why. It was time to pull back
from this new obsession. Surely there was time to
recover, and think about what she'd accomplished, to
contemplate the stories, whether they proved
anything, or just a distraction, easing her concerns
over her career path.

    She also hoped that she would be able to sort out
the conflicting images in her head. She knew what was
written in the new story, but it felt incomplete, and it
felt far too familiar for something made up in a fever
dream inspired by a random prompt.

    She headed for the bedroom. She needed to find
Jen. Except, Jen was nowhere to be found. The bed
gave off the vague sense that it had been slept in.
There was a hint of Jen's perfume in the air. The
closet was open, but it was always open. Andrea
gathered clothes and dressed quickly. She stepped
back into the hall and glanced outside. Jen's blue

Subaru was in the drive, right where it always was. . . but where was Jen?

She knew she needed to eat more, drink more water, get out into the fresh air, but she couldn't quit thinking about Jen. She was always there. Always. Had some line been crossed, or was she delusional *and* dehydrated? Was something wrong that she'd been too focused on other things to notice?

She returned to the kitchen, poured another cup of coffee and carried it to the front porch. The car was still in the drive. It occurred to her that Jen might be out for a run, so she finished the coffee and headed for the park. It was only two blocks, and there was almost always a hotdog stand on the street. Her stomach growled, and she managed a short laugh.

Andrea waved at Gladys across the street. Gladys was a schoolteacher, and absolutely obsessed with her yard. She was planting something beneath her front window. For the fleetest moment, Andrea wondered if Gladys might be planting something more than gladiolas. A hidden camera? Some sort of microphone? Then Gladys waved and returned the smile, and the notion passed. Andrea continued to the park. The closer she got, the more people she saw. Joggers, couples walking hand in hand, enjoying the sunshine. Everything she saw reminded her of Jen, and she hurried her steps.

The hotdog stand was on the corner, just like always. Andrea scanned the park, but there was no sign of Jen. She shrugged it off. A couple of hotdogs with the works in hand, and a medium diet Dr. Pepper helped calm her nerves. It was ridiculous to worry about Jen. She was an adult. She had a life beyond the house, and a single day of not being there when Andrea woke was hardly a five-alarm emergency. It wasn't Jen who spaced out at a computer for hours at a time. There was absolutely no reason to worry, and everything would be sorted out before bedtime.

She finished her food and drink and headed for home. Out of the corner of her eye, she caught a flash of light blue and turned. She knew Jen's wardrobe as well as her own. Her favorite running shirt was light blue. The flash faded even as she turned. No one was there, but Andrea's skin grew cold and damp. The hotdogs suddenly felt heavy in her stomach, and she turned toward home, walking faster and faster until *she* was running. The streets were empty, most people off to offices and day jobs. She saw one lone dog through the links of a fence, watching her pass. It felt as if she was being judged.

* * *

Jen's car was gone when she returned. Andrea hurried into the house. She stopped by the bedroom, and saw an indentation on the bed, where someone had been sitting. She continued to the bathroom and saw Jen's running clothes beside her own discarded shirt and jeans on the floor. The mirror was fogged.

Frustrated, she returned to her office. She logged

on and opened her e-mail. There were only a few messages in the Robin account, and one was from Melinda at *The Edge,* but she ignored it for the moment. What caught her eye, and what she couldn't believe she hadn't seen before, was the deleted mail folder. There were 2016 deleted emails, but she'd only read a couple of dozen. She opened it and began to read.

Dear Robin,

I can't sleep. We signed an HOA agreement, and there is a man down the street who is always in his yard. He has cameras set up and is always asking the neighborhood to link their cameras with his network. I've seen strange lights, and he has a lot of "guests" – what should I do?

Dear Robin,

My husband is digging a pit in our backyard. He is spending our life savings on a bunker, and there is actual barbed wire on top of our back fence. He wants to get a big dog, and I'm allergic.

There were more. Hundreds more. All of them seemed to believe she could solve their problems. She opened the website that Jen had created and was shocked to see that the story they had posted had two hundred fifty-three thousand reads and so many comments she didn't bother to try and read them.

What the hell? she thought.

She returned to the e-mail, clicked on the message from Melinda.

Robin,

I absolutely love this story. You can feel him disintegrating. Such insight into invisible lives, those who feel forgotten. Like your other story, it seems to reach into my mind and tug on emotions I didn't realize were just waiting for something to connect with.

Congratulations on the reactions on your website, but, in case no one ever told you, don't read the comments. Too much crazy in the world looking for an outlet. Your work really touches people deeply. The reactions are powerful.

I will be sending you the aforementioned honorarium and publishing this story immediately. Our standard contract is attached, such as it is. I'll need an address and phone number for tax purposes, and to verify that this is the right e-mail address for you to receive payments.

Thank you so much for trusting me with your work.

Melinda

Andrea opened the contract, filled it in, using her post office box for an address, saved it and then hit reply.

. . .

Melinda,

I appreciate the kind words. I hope that the story will reach some people, and that they will enjoy it. This is happening very quickly for me. Your contract is fine, and it's attached.

Yours,

Robin

Next, she did a search on Robin Orestad. The screen filled with over five million hits. She scrolled through without clicking on any. Some were about her story. Others were from conspiracy sites, trying to figure out who she was, where she was. A lot were about the crazed reactions the story was causing around the country.

Entire neighborhoods were in turmoil. At least three people in completely different locations had been shot by neighbors, and there was an article in one online magazine equating her story to some sort of government mind control experiment, created by AI to be weaponized by the deep state behind the US government. She slammed the lid of the laptop and pushed away from the desk.

"What. . . the actual fuck," she said softly.

She heard a sound behind her. She rose and literally ran out of the room toward the front door. It was closed. Jen's shoes were inside, just to one side, where she left them to protect the carpet. They hadn't been there when Andrea returned. She spun and ran to the kitchen. There was an empty folded grocery bag on the counter beside the refrigerator. The coffee cups were in the sink, rinsed. There was no sign of Jen.

Next, she tried the bedroom, then the bathroom and finally the garage. She opened the automatic door and stepped into the driveway. No one was in sight, but when she touched the hood of the car, it was still warm. She ran back inside, not bothering to close the door and completed a second high-speed lap of the house. No one. Everywhere she looked there were subtle signs, but as she continued rushing about, they faded. Where she'd seen something a moment before, it was gone, the shoes were in the closet, as if they'd never been worn. The coffee cups were in the cabinet. In the bathroom, only her clothes were strewn across the floor.

Jen's laptop was on the kitchen table. Andrea tapped a key, and the screen opened. No passwords for Jen; the two of them went through one another's computers all the time. It still felt like an intrusion, since she had the nagging sensation something was wrong, might have *been* wrong. Something she was missing.

Andrea checked Jen's history. It was strange. There were links to maps, local business organizations. She found at least half a dozen downloaded applications and HOA agreements for nearby neighborhoods. And there were links to both the Robin Orestad site, and *The Edge*, which made Andrea wonder if Jen had already known about the site, or if she'd gone there after she deleted all of those strange emails.

What is... happening? she thought.

Not knowing what else to do, she returned to her office and sat down. The manuscript Jen had printed was still sitting there, stacked neatly. She picked it up, and she began to read. As she did, the words ate their way into her mind. She read the name Jackson and it blurred. The letters rearranged and she saw Jen. Every time she read "Pastor Grimes," it felt wrong. But something was there. Something else she could not draw from her memory, and that would not leave her alone. She closed her eyes, blinked to focus, but the further she read, the stranger she felt. She shivered, and her brow grew heavy with cold sweat. When she reached the end, she threw the papers across the room and rose.

She screamed Jen's name, running from room to room again, faster, and faster. Every time she passed through, there was less of Jen. Her clothing disappeared. Photos of the two of them changed or were gone. Or had she not paid attention, and they had been moved? Had Jen changed them out, shifted things that Andrea hadn't noticed? Furniture seemed to be in different positions, or the wrong room.

Andrea stopped dead center in the kitchen, threw back her head, and screamed. Her eyes were closed, and she fought viciously for an image that was fading. Jen's face, her voice, her scent and...

...the phone rang. They had a landline, antiquated

as it was. The previous owner had installed the security system, and it required the connection. They could have upgraded it. There was a newer system with a 5G connection, but it had never seemed important. Almost no one had the number, and those who did never called it. The world had moved on to smartphones and texts years back, and on a landline, you could get on the no-call lists and prevent most of the endless spam about healthcare and real-estate.

The echoes of her scream faded as her mind registered the new sound. Loud, shrill, and somehow old. Like a memory from some other time. She knew there was something she was forgetting, some other time, some place. . . someone. She tried to concentrate, but the ringing was too loud, and too insistent. She walked across to the vintage princess phone hanging on the wall and lifted the receiver.

"Hello?"

"Andrea?"

She hesitated. She knew the voice, it was Sylvia, but the phone felt alien in her hand, and she didn't want to lose her train of thought.

"Sylvia. Why are you calling on the landline? When have you *ever?* I almost didn't answer."

"Well, you didn't answer your other number, and I've been trying for days. Where have you been? Is there something wrong?" After a hesitation. "Are you. . . working?"

Andrea leaned forward until her forehead smacked into the wall. She stayed that way, trying to clear her mind, trying to wash away the phone call and the words and in particular the "I don't really care where you've been, but are you making me more money" fake concern.

She didn't pull back from the wall, but she brought the phone up and spoke very softly.

"This is not a good time. I will call you when there is something to say. Please don't use the landline."

Then she hung up the phone and stood.

She turned and left the kitchen, made her way down the hall, and entered her office. There was a manuscript, stacked neatly, beside the keyboard. That was wrong, she knew she hadn't printed it, but there it was. She shook her head and ignored it. She glanced at the title page. There was no title, just the pseudonym. It was the story she'd just written. She remembered it now, every word. She remembered that she'd titled it. Why she would print it without that title was another thing that made absolutely no sense. She had a fleeting vision of pages scattered across the floor but shook it off.

There was a sticky note on top of the pile of pages and she reached for it. As she began to read, the letters faded. She was able to make out a "J" before it was completely blank, and she dropped it, letting it float lazily to the floor as she took her seat and logged on to the computer.

She went straight to MyWritingPrompts.com.

She logged in and waited.

The screen blinked once, and she saw the now familiar words.

WRITING ASSIGNMENT COMPLETED. PRESS ENTER
FOR THE NEXT PROMPT

She closed her eyes and hit enter. She read the word that appeared. She read the rest of the text.

FINAL PROMPT – GOOD INDEFINITELY.

She closed the browser, opened her a new document, and began to type.

"UNTITLED"

I
t was a cloudy night. There was a storm rolling in from the bay, and Teresa Vincent felt that weather to her bones. She leaned on the balcony railing of her penthouse apartment and stared down into the city, letting the yellow gleam of the street-lights and the brilliant beams of headlights fade, and her thoughts focus. She had a deadline, but for once it had not been assigned to her. It had nothing to do with headlines, or print runs, and whatever she discovered wasn't something she intended to deliver for the morning edition of the *San Valencez Beacon*. This time it was important. This time it was personal.

Her contact at the San Valencez PD, Eric Cotter, had been clear. It hadn't been long enough for the police to be seriously involved. Pamela was an adult, and she'd only been gone for a day. It wasn't even the first time. No one was going to investigate.

That much was true. Pamela had disappeared on

her plenty of times in the past, but there had always been something to hold on to. A note, or a phone message, some bit of garbage like a bus schedule, or a locker ticket from the airport. Some guy's phone number that led to a motel room, or Vegas. This time was different. This time, there was nothing. Literally. One moment Pamela had been in the office, the next she'd walked out and simply disappeared. Even the camera in the lobby hadn't caught her passing.

Teresa had built a career by following her instincts, and she'd never felt them calling to her more powerfully. Usually she was tracking city corruption, or following up on a crime SVPD was ignoring. This time she was on her own, and though she had no idea *why* she believed it, she knew her friend's life, somehow her very existence, depended on what she did next, and how quickly she did it. The thought terrified her.

Pamela was a tough cookie. She'd been a private investigator for most of her adult life, and she'd gotten in and out of some serious scrapes. What she had never done was disappear from their shared office space without her phone, her purse, or even her gun. Everything about this moment was wrong.

Teresa seated herself at Pamela's desk and stared at the blinking cursor on the login screen. The username was populated, but she needed the password, and suddenly she regretted that the two of them had never planned for a situation like this. How much of her own life was sealed away behind twelve characters and a multi-factor authentication that no one else had access to? Pamela was a near genius at research, investigation, and a hell of a proofreader, but technology mostly irritated her. She could use the computer like a champ, had a black belt in Tae Kwon Do, but the nuances of cybersecurity left her with a blank stare and texting for help.

Teresa took a deep breath and lifted the keyboard. She glanced underneath, looking for a sticky note, or a piece of folded paper. Nothing. She'd known it was too easy but had to try. She glanced around and saw a small stuffed animal resting beside a ceramic mug filled with pens and pencils. It was a bear, and it was wearing a sweater with San Valencez Dragons embroidered across the chest.

The irony that they'd put a Dragons sweater on a bear, and not a stuffed dragon, flickered momentarily through her thoughts, and was gone.

Teresa entered "Dragons" and hit enter.

"Username or password incorrect" flashed on the screen.

She frowned, then typed SVDragons.

The screen displayed "Welcome Pamela" and opened. Teresa let out the breath she'd been holding. She opened email first. There were fifteen unread messages, and the last one read was from Pamela's fiancé. There was nothing in it about plans, or directions. The new messages had all come in after the disappearance, so Teresa moved on to the calendar.

The past two days had nothing but a couple of lunch engagements and a reminder to pay for lawn service. Teresa frowned. For the second time in only a few moments, she was glad that Pamela hated technology. She continued. The first thing that popped up, the last thing that Pamela had seen, was some sort of internet literary magazine called *The Edge*. Teresa nearly passed over it, but it seemed so out of character for Pamela, she opened the page.

It was a surprisingly attractive website. The menu curved down and away from the side of a mountain, stormy skies above and beyond. There was an editorial, some book and movie reviews, and a final link that simply said "Fiction." Ignoring this, Teresa opened the editorial. It was written by a woman named Melinda Ross.

"Greetings, and welcome to the newest edition of *The Edge*. I know I've said this before, but the fiction in this issue is special. In fact, it's *so* special that we have only included a single story. That's right. Just one.

Some of you will be familiar with the name Robin Orestad. Her story "Words," posted on her own website, has gone viral. If the comments are to be believed (never read the comments) people have gone crazy over that story. And I don't mean they really love it. I mean they have gone bat-shit, over the top crazy. They've lost homes, relationships, even their lives. After I read the story, I did some research on those comments. I tracked some of the stories to real time, and while a lot of it is the usual troll-talk, even more of it seems to be true, at least on the surface. Think about that. A story so powerfully written it's changed thousands of lives. And if Ms. Orestad is to be believed, it's her first published work.

I digress. I'm not here to talk about that story. If you want to read it, you can find her website and about a million and a half search hits while you're at it. There are entire video channels dedicated to tracking her down, proving she's part of some weird government conspiracy, and documenting all of the purported effects of her work. Knock yourselves out.

What I have for you is story number two. Never published, never read, until now. Of course, I've read it, and I'll tell you. . . there are a lot of you out there who are going to relate to Jackson. Just don't let it get weird, okay? I don't want the FBI breaking down my doors because you can't handle a short story – even a very powerful one. Enough from me, though. Go. Read. The title of this gem? "Shunned."

Melinda Ross

Teresa clicked on the story and was about to start reading when she thought better of it. Instead, she scrolled down to the comments. It had been two days since "Shunned" was posted, but there were already two thousand five hundred posts, and a crazy number of shares.

Meghan56:

Please help me? My daughter is missing. Just gone. I found her computer was still turned on. Her password was written on a sticky note under the keyboard. It was open to this page, to this story...

Caleb J

They don't see me either. None of them. They don't know I'm alive. I could walk out into the street and wait to be hit by a bus and if it happened, they would call someone to clean the street and be back at their phones and newspapers as if it never happened. As if I never happened. How did you know?

There were so many more. The comments were equally split between those who had lost someone, and those who felt themselves lost, forgotten, or shunned. There were also a few comments from people who'd read the other story, the viral one that had started this author on her viral ride. These were mostly warnings or calls to the author to reach out.

Nothing pointed to Pamela specifically, but this was exactly the kind of website that would have interested her. There was a story here, something that, so far, had not hit any of the mainstream media outlets. Maybe something important. Even considering the number of comments that were probably trolls or copycats, the missing, if this was real, would have to number in the hundreds, and when she refreshed the page, she saw the number had jumped by at least another five hundred. Teresa blinked. She heard about things going viral all the time, but this was the first time she'd seen the phenomenon in real time. So fast. So many connections.

Teresa started searching for information on the author. There wasn't much; a single website, and all of the hits pointing to that site, but following the name led to nothing that made sense. There were other Robin Orestads, but none who seemed likely to be the owner of the website. There was an author's photo, but when she ran it through an image search, she came up with several stock photo sites offering images for commercial use. Whoever the author was, she didn't want to be found, and she'd left a very small digital footprint. As far as the internet was concerned, she didn't really exist. Never had.

Shifting tacks, Teresa did a search of the magazine editor, Melinda Ross. This proved slightly more helpful, but only slightly. She popped up as a username on a lot of varied sites. None of them was a personal home page, or a biography, but it wasn't as clean as the Robin Orestad identity. One thing the two seemed to have in common was that they were manufactured. The second thing was more interesting. The IP address for the magazine, and that of the web page for the author, shared an internet service provider. Both were private – there was no direct contact for a webmaster, but the IP addresses were from the same block, and that alone was enough to be suspect.

She shifted back to the comments section. The most recent entry was from Andrea S:

. . .

This message is for Jen. I know that I have not paid the attention to you that you deserve. I know that every day I selfishly do whatever helps me and that you support me every time. You advise me. You explain things to me that I don't get, and I go ahead and do whatever I was going to do as if that never happened. I am that person. I am guilty. But I am also lonely, and broken, and I need you back!

I didn't know this story was about you. I didn't know involving you in it would take you away from me. I didn't know so many felt forgotten and invisible, and I thought my own concerns were the only ones that were important. That I could validate the fame and the money, that I could create something real, or meaningful, and then I'd feel okay with the endless formulaic nonsense I produce. I know it brings people pleasure. I know it fills voids for others. It used to do that for me as well, but now it mostly leaves me empty, so I thought it also left me unfulfilled.

Until you weren't here, and I realized that the only thing standing between me, and that fulfillment, was myself. I had everything I needed, and, if you read this – if you can find your way back – I will be here. There was another writing prompt, and I'm working on it. There is no time limit, but I've been writing at a crazy pace. Maybe if I get the words right, and the story, we'll be able to laugh about all of this later.

I miss you. . .

    -Andrea

· · ·

Teresa read over this message a second time. Something was off about it, and something about the name seemed far too familiar, and the style of the writing, the intimacy, stood out. It wasn't like the other comments. It didn't seem directed at the magazine, or even the story. It didn't fit, and a long life of journalistic curiosity had taught her that the things that didn't fit, loose threads, breaks in a pattern, were where the secrets would be found. She didn't know how, or why she knew, but she had a feeling that the two disappearances weren't a coincidence, considering the comments on the story. She thought, just maybe, that this note was going to lead her to Pamela.

After the tone and message of that one note, she was glad she'd ignored the body of the story. There was regret and guilt in those words she could not deal with at the moment, though they tugged at her heart. What she had done with her career, what she'd accomplished, would never have been possible without Pamela's help. She had to focus on that. She couldn't afford to let some crazy online story drag her down a dark well of emotions and prevent her from thinking clearly.

She thought about calling Ken, Pamela's fiancé, then thought better of it. There was no sense in upsetting him at this point. He was in Chicago on business, so there was no chance Pamela was with him. There would be plenty of time for an explanation later when she had one.

The first thing to do was to find out who Andrea

was, and to figure out what she'd meant by "another writing prompt." Maybe Andrea knew who Robin Orestad was, or maybe she could provide a clue that would lead to Melinda Ross. Could it all be connected even more directly? Cotter, a computer geek who worked in the forensics lab downtown owed her a favor, and it was time to collect.

She took her laptop and headed out into the street. She didn't have time to call and make an appointment. It was time for a visit to her favorite precinct of the SVPD and hope for a miracle.

*   *   *

"It's not very well hidden," Cotter said, clicking keys and flipping through a series of searches and web pages. "The magazine is very well designed, but it's on a standard do-it-yourself type of platform, like a newer version of PagePress. The code is basically the same for all of the users, and while a lot of things are private, others aren't. You just have to know where to look, what to find, and what to do with it once it's found."

"English, Cotter."

He grinned. Eric Cotter was about five feet five inches with black framed glasses like the ones they issue in the military. He had short, curly brown hair and a grin that made him look more like a hillbilly than a forensics tech. He was wearing that grin now.

"Andrea, who left the comment, has commented

on a lot of other sites using that same account. There is a record of everything users with an account post so they can go back and follow up on replies or make further posts of their own. Mostly she compliments the sites of authors, but the posts are strange. They have a sort of familiarity most fans or trolls couldn't pull off."

"What do you mean?"

"She knows them," Cotter said. "She knows all of these authors, and this last post confirms it."

He stepped back so Teresa could see. The open page for a romantic suspense author Teresa knew. Bridgette Barnes. The comment itself was innocuous.

"Loved this last one. Can't wait to see where you send Lindsay next!"

What got Teresa's heart beating was the reply from the author. "I have *Forget Me Not* on my TBR page. We should get together next month, after I have a chance to dig in."

Cotter reached past her and flipped to another tab. It was open to author Andrea Simmons. Centered at the top was the cover of her newest book. *Forget Me Not* – just announced. There was also a link for fans and reviewers to download an excerpt ahead of time. Teresa scanned the description of the novel and felt a wave of dizziness wash through her.

"What the. . . ?"

She turned to Cotter. "Do you know the author? The books?"

Cotter shook his head. "Never heard of her, but this is the ninth in the series."

He flipped over to the page listing previous books and scanned the reviews.

"That's strange," he said.

"Stranger than a series of books I have never heard of that seem to feature me?"

"No, but look." He pointed at the bottom of the listing for each of the other books. There were prices, ISBN numbers, and publication dates for each. "There has been a steady stream of books, one a year, for the last eight years. Look at the publication date on that last one."

It was only a month before.

"But how. . . she wrote another book in a month?"

"It seems pretty odd to announce a book almost a full year ahead of publication. She may still be writing it. It is strange, though. I mean, they already have cover art. She might have been writing ahead all along, but it's definitely weird the way it's being marketed. And that title. The story you told me about, the disappearances. Is that a coincidence?"

"No such thing," Teresa said. "Coincidences are just patterns that merge unexpectedly. They will distract you if you let them, but it's best to take facts at face value and follow threads to their end."

"When did you become a philosopher?"

"When did I become the heroine of a romantic thriller series? I'm a woman of many talents."

Cotter sat down, clicked through a few more pages, then printed a single page.

"It's her address, phone number, and her agent's number. She has an assistant. Want to guess what her name is?"

"If it's not Jen, I will be deeply disappointed."

Cotter grinned and gave her the page. "You'd better let me know how this one turns out."

"Maybe you should read the book." Teresa grinned, took the sheet of paper, and headed for the door. It was late, but she wasn't about to sleep on this. Andrea Simmons' home was across town in one of the ritzier neighborhoods near the beach. It was time for a visit.

Cotter started to reply, then, instead, clicked the excerpt from *Forget Me Not* and sent it to his tablet. It was late, he was tired, but his curiosity, as always, got the best of him.

* * *

Teresa drove her Mustang slowly into the neighborhood where Andrea Simmons lived, taking in details as she passed. There was a park with a running trail that rounded a small retention pond. The streets were neat and clean, the homes different hued versions of one another. All of the cars were new, and most were garaged. It was the kind of neighborhood that took their HOAs very seriously. There were no forgotten trash cans lining the street, no ragged yards or unsightly lawn ornaments. Well, except for one lady who seemed to believe you could replace sod with lawn gnomes, and a house with a privacy fence not hiding a very abandoned looking car half-concealed by a tarp. It was the kind of place you mostly saw on television dramas, or in movies. Teresa hated it instantly.

It felt wrong. All of it. She'd lived in San Valencez, California all of her adult life. She'd been up and down the streets, crawled through alleys and gotten drunk in dive bars chasing stories. It was her home. Turning into the driveway of the home she sought, all of the hairs stood up on her arms. Nothing felt real. It was as if someone had staged it for her. Everything was perfect. There wasn't a single detail that felt 'off' in the image of the entire neighborhood or this home in particular.

And it felt familiar. That was worse. She looked out the window of her Mustang toward the walk winding around to the front door and swore she'd walked it a thousand times. She was certain she'd find that the casing around the doorbell was cracked, the doormat would be scuffed, "Welcome" faded until it was barely legible. More than anything she ever wanted, she needed to put the car in reverse, back out of the driveway and disappear into the city, forgetting any of this had happened. Then she thought about Pamela and Jen, whoever that was, and avoiding bookstores for the rest of her life.

She couldn't do it. For some reason, the cover of the book she'd seen on the laptop screen flashed into her thoughts. That title, *Forget Me Not*, brought a second image to the surface. Pamela. Dark jeans, bright blue eyes, and her head tilted to one side, like a dog who'd picked up an interesting scent. That was the essence of her friend. That was what she stood to lose. She had to see this through.

She cut the engine and climbed out. A single bulb burned on the porch, directly above the front door.

Like always, she thought. Then she mentally slapped herself.

She stepped onto the porch and reached for the doorbell, but the door opened before she could press it. She stood very still as it swung inward. A woman stood there, long, strawberry blonde hair pulled back in a ponytail, thin glasses dropped slightly over her nose. The woman's eyes were intense, taking in every inch of Teresa as if she didn't trust her eyes.

"Andrea?" Teresa said. "My name is. . ."

"Teresa Vincent," the woman said. "I know. I. . . I'm sorry. Please come in."

It was like walking into a surreal dream. The rooms, the hall, the furniture. She knew it, and at the same time, she knew she had never been in this place before. She had never met this woman, never heard of her, or of her books, but she knew which room was the bedroom, that there was an office at the end of the hall, and even though it was very late, there would be fresh coffee brewed. She smelled it, and that single, powerful scent nearly drove her scrambling back to the door. She felt like a rabbit who'd walked into some sort of strange trap, and though she'd come with a thousand questions, she had no idea what to say.

She followed Andrea into the kitchen, where she found that two cups were already waiting on the table.

"Were you expecting. . . ?"

"You? Of course."

She poured coffee into both cups, added a single spoon of sugar to her own, but nothing at all to Teresa's.

"Black, as always?"

Teresa nodded numbly. "But how. . . ?"

Andrea handed her the coffee and turned away without speaking. She left the kitchen and turned down the hall. Teresa followed. They passed a bedroom, and she nearly stopped to glance inside. The door to the office was open. There was a desk with twin monitors and a desktop computer against one wall. On the opposite wall was a bookcase. All the shelves were full, but there was one central section set off from the rest.

Teresa crossed over and read the titles.

On the Edge of Forever

Lost Memories

She slid her gaze across to the end. The last volume was *Imagine Us in Heaven*.

She turned. Andrea stood by the computer, holding a manuscript in her hands, and smiling wanly.

"You're probably looking for this. I'm afraid it's not finished, but there is plenty of time before publication. Unless you ask my agent."

Teresa stepped closer and held out her hand. Andrea peeled off a number of pages and handed over the rest.

Teresa scanned the first few paragraphs, stopped, glanced up at Andrea, and then continued.

The manuscript began at the moment she'd realized that Pamela was missing.

"What the hell?"

"Read. Please?"

Teresa began scanning the pages quickly. It was all there, the password, the conversation with Cotter, the web page. She glanced up, then back down, and saw the words. . . "Teresa glanced up in shock."

The papers fell from her fingers, and she took a step back, half turning toward the door. "Who are you?" she asked. "What is this? This place. . . that!" She pointed at the scattered pages on the floor.

"Your life," Andrea said. "My life. My work. I thought I was wasting it all, that there was nothing to it, but you. You are so. . . real."

"I would say you're starting to sound crazy, lady," Teresa said, "but that ship sailed a while back. What have you been doing, stalking me? Do you have cameras in my home? Where is Pamela?"

"And who is Robin Orestad?"

"I thought you'd have figured that much out by now. There is no Robin. I wrote the stories. I wrote them because I thought my work wasn't serious. Because it wasn't enough for me that people loved the novels – that they loved *you*. I thought I had to prove something, and so, I ignored everyone. I ignored my agent. I ignored my fans. I ignored Jen, even while she supported me in doing so, and she is gone. Like your Pamela.

"But nothing is as it seems. You read the editorial at *The Edge*. . . What you don't know is, there is no Melinda Ross. There isn't really even a magazine called *The Edge*. It was Jen all along. She knew what I needed, what I wanted, so she built it for me. Created an outlet. I don't know if she knew what would happen, where it would lead.

"Let me show you something."

Andrea turned and seated herself at the computer. She logged on and opened the web browser. Despite the absolute dread chilling her blood, Teresa stepped forward and watched over the woman's shoulder.

The website she opened was a very simple one. My Writing Prompts. The screen was blank except for a button that said LOGIN. Andrea clicked on the button.

A single line of text appeared.

PROMPT COMPLETE.

Nothing else.

"What is it?" Teresa said. "What does it mean?"

"The first thing this website asked me was, 'Are you a talented writer?' It was a trap. My entire purpose in seeking this site was to prove something I already knew. What Jen already knew. What I should have just accepted. I was always good enough. I simply could not bring myself to believe in it. In you. Do you know how many adventures we've shared, you and I?"

"Exactly none," Teresa said, backing away again.

"Where were you born?" Andrea asked sharply.

"Lavender, California. 1972."

Andrea closed the writing prompt site and typed Lavender, California into a search engine.

There were, as Teresa had expected, pages of hits. But none of them showed a map, or a community page. None of them involved real estate or schools. They all led to a single name, Andrea Simmons. There were images of the books, images of book signings, videos of television interviews.

"Your first memory is from 1996," Andrea said without looking up. "Your first big story, do you remember?"

"Of course, I do, but. . ."

"You solved the mystery of seven missing women. They would have been taken away, sold to slavery in some far-off place, but you found them."

Teresa turned and stared at the books on the bookshelf again. "*On the Edge of Forever*," she said.

Andrea smiled. "Yes. . ."

"But. . ." Teresa scrambled for the pages on the floor, but they were impossibly jumbled. "But I. . ."

"Those pages don't matter," Andrea said, shaking the rest of the pages she still held. "They have already happened. They are a recording. You can read them a hundred times, but you already know every word. They already happened. It's why you are here. *I* am why you are here. These," she held out the rest of what Teresa had believed to be a manuscript. "These matter."

The pages were blank.

* * *

Cotter frowned at the screen. He had started reading and hadn't been able to pull away since Teresa left his office. It was crazy. In the book, she had also left, then driven across town to Andrea Simmons' home. There were hints of déjà vu and he almost felt her hesitation in the description, her desire to turn and run, and her inability to follow through on that thought.

As weird as that had all been, what he hadn't been prepared for was the presentation of the blank pages, in a book he'd purchased and downloaded from the internet. . . or the words that slowly began scrolling across the screen a moment later. At the same time, he began to read again, the story picked up with Teresa noticing new words appearing on a blank page, knocking them out of Andrea's hands so they scattered again, and running.

"Find her," Andrea screamed. "Find *them!*"

The words kept scrolling, but Cotter rose and headed down the hall. He grabbed a fresh cup of coffee from the lounge and hit the bathroom. He didn't know why, and he didn't even begin to understand how, but it felt important that he get back to his desk, catch up with the story, and read along. He couldn't do anything directly to change what was happening, short of calling Teresa and distracting her, but he would be seeing the narrator's voice. That meant that it was possible he would sometimes know things sooner than she did, and maybe, if he was careful, he could do something useful. Something important.

As he slid back into his chair, he had the sinking sensation he'd see those last thoughts recorded in black and white, right up to the description of the scene, and his realization that his thoughts could be recorded. It made him dizzy, and he closed his eyes to focus. It gave him just a few seconds where, like Schrödinger's cat, he was a free, thinking being, or a character in a story with no control over his own fate. Then he opened his eyes and began to read as quickly as he could take in the words, trying to catch up, maybe get a second ahead, and take a shot at being the hero.

* * *

Teresa tore out of Andrea's driveway without even looking for traffic. She shot back down the road toward the city, mind racing. She knew she should be careful, that she needed to calm down and think, but another part of her mind had raced ahead, thinking about the blank pages, and wondering—if she was the protagonist of a novel—could she actually be hurt, or killed? How would getting a ticket, or being in a car crash move the story along? Every thought she had, every small clue that occurred to her was followed by the realization that it might not be her own thought at all, and that even thinking about the thoughts could be a plot device. It was nearly enough to make her turn head-on into a tree and see how things played out. Nearly.

There had to be an answer. If she could be snatched out of her life and dropped into some sort of surreal fictional world, she could also find her way out. The events of the past half hour were already blurring. Her mind rationalized it as hallucinations, and her need to compartmentalize and get to work had begun to suppress it all and concentrate. In the end, it didn't matter. Pamela was missing. If Andrea was to be believed, so was Jen, but also, Jen was involved. That meant the keys were either in the magazine site, the stories, or the site with the writer's prompts, possibly a combination of the three.

With a great effort, she slowed her breathing, slowed to the speed limit, and pressed the button on her steering wheel to activate her phone.

"Call Cotter," she said.

There was only one ring before she heard his frantic voice. "I know. Don't waste time, or words. I am reading this. I *think* there is a possibility that there will be points where what I read hasn't happened yet. I don't know whose words they are."

"Does it matter?"

"Of course, it matters. If someone is manipulating this, we can find them. If something is simply recording what we're doing, we are in control. Either way, we have two missing persons to locate."

Teresa gritted her teeth. "Chase the lady from the website. If she's really someone named Jen, she may have manipulated the entire thing. I'll see if I can figure out what happened to Pamela. I am going to pull over and read that first story. It was the last thing in her browsing history. Then I'm going to check out that writing prompt site and see if it's a real thing."

"Be careful. Guess I don't have to tell you there is something really strange going on here. . . or there. . . or. . ."

"Cotter," Teresa said. "Shut up."

She hung up the phone, hit the gas, and turned onto the freeway, racing for home. She thought about the speed limit exactly once, while whispering "fuck it," under her breath. If she got arrested, she was probably experiencing a long-term hallucination, and it would be good to know that. Cotter could probably get her out on bail. No one ever got a ticket in a novel except in stories where the local law-enforcement had been infiltrated by the antagonist, and this wasn't that kind of story. At least, it didn't seem to be."

She hit her exit at twice the speed limit, ignored the light at the end, and roared on toward home. There was no traffic. There were no police.

* * *

Cotter reached under his desk, pulled his personal laptop out of its case, and fired it up. There was a guest network the precinct used for personal devices and visitors. He didn't want his next series of searches going through the standard firewall logs. Someone might still check the guest history, but he doubted it. Despite the department's "hard stance" on cybersecurity, he knew there was only so much you could monitor and analyze and still maintain operations, and he was on good terms with all of those being underpaid to maintain the networks. Even if something popped up on a search, he was pretty sure they'd let him slide. If not, he was equally certain, at this point, that it didn't matter.

He opened an anonymous browser window, typed in a URL he would erase from his history, as always, the second he was done using it, and waited for the login prompt. The internet was a layered construct. Most of the world ran on what he called layer one. Commercial pages, social media, and commerce. The layers were all connected, but it was a one-way connection. The deeper levels, and there were a lot of them, were filled with people with, as Liam Neeson would say, a particular set of skills. Not everything on the *dark web* was dark, but all of it was dangerous. There were chat sites, data dumps, private servers, all available if you had gained the proper level of trust, and respect. Not just anyone could achieve either. The site he needed was a deep search that bypassed a number of security protocols and provided results the

FBI would be jealous of. He entered his username, and, as usual, smiled. It was a variation on his cat's name. She was a Persian named Iris (he called her Boots). The username was Nanabootz. His password was a combination of letters and numbers that sort of spelled out "trust no one" because it was a reminder how true that motto became as you delved deeper.

He wasn't going to find the person behind *The Edge* on a "whois" search, or by tracing the ISP behind the IP number. Nothing on the internet was ever really gone, and very little was actually secure. It just depended on the level of skill, the value of information, and what you were looking for.

It wasn't Cotter's first rodeo. There had been plenty of times when, hampered by regulations and protocol, he'd slipped information into investigations that no one had ever questioned, but that he'd obtained by means beyond the borders of the legal. He hated it. He hated being a part of it, hated pretending to buddy up to people who would ruin someone's life with a few clicks on the keyboard, but it was one of those cases where the ends absolutely justified the means. It sort of went back to that old idiom about good people standing by and doing nothing.

This time he didn't hesitate. What would they ask him? "Did you attempt to obtain personal details on a woman running an electronic magazine titled *The Edge?*"

There was nothing illegal about such a search, at least on the surface, and there would be no record of the deeper search he actually initiated. He would make sure to use all of the standard tools as well, and come up with something he could point to, offer some technobabble about, and ease any doubt. The fact it might be the last search he ever made removed any reluctance he might have felt.

Surprisingly, it took only a matter of seconds to retrieve the results he needed. Cotter frowned. He had been scraping information out of the dark corners of the web for a very long time. It was always a puzzle, always more complex than standard searches. The ease of this search left him feeling somehow cheated. He thought about the words, scrolling out across the pages of the eBook he'd left open in another window. A pet peeve of his was authors, or writers for film or television, who couldn't be bothered to research details about computer-related skills. He glanced at the screen again, half-expecting it to turn into a monochrome black background with green ascii characters flashing by like his *Matrix* screensaver.

He sent the results of the search to his printer, then pushed back from the desk. If he'd seen this in a movie, he'd have cursed and ranted at anyone close enough to listen. He'd have told them it doesn't work like that, it's a lot more complicated, and it takes time. He stared at the screen, thought about re-running the search, or digging deeper to be certain someone hadn't hacked in and skewed the results. Then he leaned forward, logged out, and stood. He went to the printer and picked up the pages.

He carried them back to his desk and sat, thinking back to earlier times when he'd created similar searches, and tried to remember the problems, the complexities. He knew it had never been like this, and yet now those memories were fuzzy and incomplete, like he'd read them somewhere, or seen them in a TV drama where he recalled the plot, but not the details. He closed his eyes, cleared his mind, and started to read. Absolutely nothing would be gained by trying to second guess the search. It was remotely possible that someone had outmaneuvered him and inserted results. No matter how good you were with code or security, there was always someone better. The kids just starting out had most of what you already knew available to them. Dwayne Johnson had nailed it in that stupid movie *The Tooth Fairy.* "Lower your expectations."

The Edge had been online for about a year. It had started as a blog, and the early posts had all been the work of a single person. There were essays, a few poems, a couple of short stories. The author's name was Jenifer Manske. The web page contained few biographical notes, but the deeper search had turned up contact information. Familiar contact information.

There was a second website connected to Jenifer Manske, though more obscurely. The URL was mywritingprompts.com.

Jenifer Manske was employed as the personal assistant to author Andrea Simmons. Her residence was the same as Andrea's, but she had her own phone.

Publicly there were no connections between the blog, the magazine, and her position with Simmons, but it was clear there was more than a business relationship between the two. There were only two bedrooms in the Simmons home, and he knew from Teresa's visit that one of them was an office.

He continued to read. At one point, he stopped and ran back to his computer. He hadn't read the stories the first time he'd visited, but suddenly he felt compelled. One of the documents that had come up in the search was an HOA agreement. The neighborhood was only one street removed from the Simmons home. He vaguely remembered that the comments on the first story, "The Word," had been full of mentions of HOA rules. There had to be a connection.

He clicked the link and began to read.

* * *

Teresa sat in front of her computer, staring at a blank text box on the screen. The questions, "Create an Account?" and "Are you a talented writer?"—and her answer—had passed. The prompt read, "ENTER SAMPLE." Beneath that it said, "Write what you want to say to the world."

Her words were confined to facts. She investigated; she recorded what she learned. She uncovered things that needed to be uncovered and presented them to the world. It had been a long time since she'd written anything personal. Considering all the recent discoveries, she wondered if she had ever written anything at all. It was hard to shake that off. She had read the two stories by Robin Orestad. They were bleak, dark, and unrelenting glimpses into the same sort of realities she had dedicated her life to reporting on. Something told her that sort of thing was not what the website was after, and as ridiculous as it seemed, she also felt that if she failed to deliver the proper input, the site would shut her down, and a valuable resource would be lost. She closed her eyes, took a deep breath, then began to type.

There are many ways to perceive reality, and all of them depend on knowledge and understanding that is impossible to attain. Every person lives in a tiny bubble world painted by thoughts, perceptions, conceits. The close-in details are clear and comfortable, but the farther the bubble expands, growing ethereal and intersecting with the outer reaches of other bubbles, the fuzzier those details become.

In those intersections, a massive, deceitful vision held together by coincidence, similar tastes and dreams, and nearly overwhelming insecurity is the real world. The one we all pretend to believe in, even though there are no two people, and no two worlds, exactly alike. It's our super-power, and our weakness.

My writing may be intuitive and clever, inspired and beautiful, but it's just as possible I'm a character in someone else's story, being written a few words ahead and drawing me along like the rabbit in a dog race, rushing just far enough ahead to ensure I follow. The words could be mine, or yours, or simply a translation, or interpretation of words slipping through the outer reaches of my bubble just far enough to become my muse.

The only question, then, is do I believe in the words? Do I believe in my writing? I find that any other course, any other train of thought leads to madness. I live in my own world, my own bubble. In that space, I am the most talented writer who exists.

Without hesitation, Teresa pressed "Enter" and watched the screen. It blinked once, and a new line of text appeared. A moment later she saw the line:

ACCOUNT CREATED
PRESS ENTER FOR PROMPT

She pressed ENTER.

A single word appeared. She blinked once, twice, and it was gone.

The screen read; ACCOUNT CREATED. SUCCESS-FULLY LOGGED OFF. PROMPT VALID FOR TWENTY-FOUR HOURS.

Redemption. The prompt had flashed the single word, and for a moment it paralyzed her. What did it mean? What did she have to say about it? What did it have to do with Pamela?

She closed her eyes again and cleared her thoughts. There were a set number of facts. Two people were missing. The disappearances were in some way related to the stories written by the fictional Robin Orestad and published online by Andrea's partner, Jen. Jen was missing. Andrea was the author of a series of novels that, either miraculously, or by some creepy coincidences, mirrored Teresa's life. Pamela was also missing, and she had read the stories.

Mentally, she created a bulletin board with index cards and string. She put herself at the top of the chart and Andrea off to one side. She put the stories lower, but in between the two of them and, almost irritably, did a mental scrawl above both that was simply. . . prompts.

There were two stories. She was certain that Andrea must have received two prompts. She didn't think that those were as important as the fact that, in both stories, someone disappeared. She pictured cards with Jen and Pamela's names beside the story titles. What Cotter had discovered seemed to indicate that Jen had been more involved with the publishing of the stories than it first appeared, and she had definitely disappeared first. Given any form of reality as a basis, it would have taken time for Andrea to realize she was gone and begin working on the new novel.

Teresa dealt with facts. She didn't make up stories, she uncovered them. She put a mental number one beside Jen's name and drew a line between that and the first story. Then, almost irritated, she erased it. Something was itching at her thoughts and the connection didn't seem solid. She thought about the second story, a church filled with sanctimonious faithful who were anything but. Forgotten children, and a pastor.

She started to dial Cotter, and then pulled back. He was working and anything she tasked him with would become another distraction. Instead, did her own search for "Church of New Light"+Grimes.

The screen filled with references to services, special events, a revival that had taken place earlier in the year, funerals, and finally, just before she was about to change tactics and try a different search, an article in the *San Valencez Chronicle*.

MISSING BOY LAST SEEN AT CHURCH OF NEW LIGHT

"Last Sunday, around eleven-thirty a.m., Jackson Craig, son of Abner and Gloria Craig, went missing. The boy was last seen entering the baptismal chamber of the Church of New Light. Several members of the congregation remember him rising and joining the line to be baptized, but no one has seen him since he passed through the curtains at the top of those stairs. There are several ways in and out of that back area, but no one recalls seeing him beyond that point. Police have questioned all those who came forward during the service, as well as Pastor Grimes, the ushers, and the maintenance staff, but no clues have thus far been uncovered.

This is not the first such disappearance involving The Church of New Light. A young girl, Madeline Grace, disap-

peared from a youth picnic last spring, and another boy, JJ Brannigan, left a youth choir rehearsal two years back and never made it to the parking lot where his mother was waiting.

Detectives have not been able to connect these disappearances at this time, but investigations are ongoing. . ."

There was more, but nothing detailed. Four missing children. Teresa cleared the search and entered "Church of New Light"+Simmons.

There were several links to news stories, but one stood out. August and Leticia Simmons had made a substantial donation to the church many years back. They had, in fact, been responsible for upgrades to the very baptismal pool in the story. They had been members of the congregation for over a decade. The article said they had a daughter, Andrea, who had just graduated high school and was to attend San Valencez University that fall. That was the only mention of Andrea, but it placed her at that church as a child.

It also placed her there during the period when Jackson Craig had disappeared. Andrea would have been a couple of years older than the boy, but they must have crossed paths. Even a cursory examination of the articles mentioning the church showed a very active youth ministry.

There were only a couple of pieces of the puzzle evading her. Where had Jackson gone? The boy disappeared from a church full of people and was never seen again. Clearly Andrea either knew what had happened, or suspected. Impossible to know if she'd written the story from memory, or if she'd just known the boy and how he felt. Maybe it was guilt. In the story, Jackson had been all but invisible to those around him. She would have been a part of that, might even have spoken to him or heard him speaking to someone else, but hadn't reached out. Not that it was her place to do so, but no one gets to choose which memories will haunt them.

She checked her watch. She still had eighteen hours. It wasn't far to the church. She thought, maybe, if she could find a way to get inside, or even just check the exterior, she might figure out how someone could disappear. Or possibly, and more likely, how they could *be* disappeared from a church in broad daylight.

Before she logged off, she ran one more search. She searched for Jackson's parents, Abner, and Gloria. There were a surprising number of hits, and one in particular caught her eye. About one month after their son had gone missing, the couple had moved to a larger home. It seemed Abner had inherited a considerable sum from a distant relative. The details were vague. There wasn't much after that, but there was nothing really newsworthy about the couple. The big event of their life had been the loss of their only son.

Frowning, she closed the browser. Something bothered her about the last story, but she couldn't place it. Such a strange, tragic story, and just as Andrea had written it, the world had forgotten Jackson Craig.

She grabbed her purse, on impulse slipping into her bedroom and opening her gun safe. She had a .38

her father had given her, and she knew how to use it, but she seldom took it out. Something told her that if there was ever going to be a good time to have it close, this was it. She tucked it in beside her wallet, slung the purse over her shoulder and headed back to the garage and her car. Outside the window the storm had abated, and the moon had risen, giving the streets a shimmering silver glow. She tried to imagine how Andrea would describe it, then shook her head to clear the thought.

Moments later she was pulling into the street and heading into the city.

* * *

The Church of New Light was an impressive edifice. The moonlight hid the beauty of the stained glass, but Teresa remembered an article in the *San Valencez Chronicle* a few years back. Some famous artist had designed the windows, and the baptismal pool. When the sun was just right, it shot scarlet light at a huge bas-relief of Jesus, trickling down toward the pool like fresh blood. She vaguely remembered earlier articles and a scandal. Paster Grimes was not the first to hold court on that hallowed ground, but none of that was relevant.

She parked a block away, not wanting to draw any unwanted attention at such a late hour. She considered just trying the front door. It seemed as if the doors of a house of God would be open at any hour.

She ignored that urge and skirted around the side of the building. She passed a side door and decided not to test that one either. It was brightly lit, and visible from the street. She turned the corner at the rear of the church and slipped up close to the wall. There was a single yellowish light hanging over a small concrete stairway and service entrance.

With a quick glance to be certain there was no one watching, she climbed down and tried the door. It was locked. She frowned, and then, she remembered the drive from Andrea's home to her own. She remembered how no matter how hard she pressed the gas, or how tightly she wound into the curves, there had been no accident. No traffic. No police to see her and pull her over and read her her rights. She reached into her purse and pulled out a small leather bag. It was a lock-pick set that Pamela had given her for Christmas. Teresa had watched the online videos and had a practice lock on her desk, but she'd never managed to make it work. She only carried them because in her line of work, being prepared for emergency situations was standard.

She pulled two of the metal picks from the pack and inserted them quickly into the lock. Thinking back to scenes she'd seen in movies, she worked them side to side, pushing and pulling, and the lock opened. She stared at it for a long moment, then opened the door and stepped inside, dropping the lockpicks back into her purse. She had never in her life wished for something to be harder than in that moment or been more relieved that it was easy. There would be time to worry over that mess once Pamela was home.

The interior of the church was dimly lit by strip lights running along the floor. They provided just enough illumination so a maintenance worker would not trip or bang into a wall. Down the hallway she saw a brighter light pooling just outside a closed door. Very slowly, and as quietly as she could manage, she crept closer, listening for any sound or sign that she'd been discovered.

The door was solid wood with an ornate crystal knob that shone with flickers of brilliance in the shadows. Teresa pressed her ear to the door and listened. There was an odd, wavering sound, but nothing like voices, or footsteps. The light beneath the door rippled. She took a deep breath and turned the knob. The door opened easily.

The light beyond the door was not centered on a single bulb, or a fluorescent panel. Shadows danced on the walls, along with flickers of rippling brilliance. It reminded her briefly of a visit she'd made to the San Valencez Aquarium. There was a room there where the overhead lighting was dimmed, and the lights within the aquariums provided the only illumination.

She stepped inside and closed the door behind her. To her left, there was a set of curtains. She stepped closer and parted them. On the far side of the curtains was another door. It was closed. She tried the knob, and it was locked. She frowned and turned back to the room. There was a short set of stairs that curved upward from the far wall. She climbed slowly, keeping a solid grip on the polished wooden handrail.

There were more curtains. Large curtains, like the ones they opened and closed at off-Broadway productions. They were closed, but she knew they would open onto the church beyond. Lights glimmered at the bottom of a pool of crystal-clear water. A pump, she assumed attached to a filter of some kind, pumped water into the pool and caused the ripples of light. It was almost hypnotic.

Teresa stood, as if staring out into a crowd of expectant churchgoers. She remembered the story. She turned and made her way back down the stairs. There was something missing, and she needed to find it. The walls were covered in ornate tapestries, and she began with the first on the left at the bottom of the stairs. She pulled it back, saw a solid wall behind it, and moved on. When she pulled back the third tapestry, she stopped. Something was different. There was a smudged spot on the pristine white plaster. She pressed her hand against that spot and moved it around slowly. Her heart nearly stopped when an audible *Click!* broke the silence.

The wall shifted inward, and an angled opening appeared. Before she could consider the implications, she pulled out her phone, opened the camera, and started a video recording. She stepped forward into darkness. She had a moment of panic as the panel slid back into place, but the phone emitted a dim glow and using that, it only took a moment of fumbling along the wall to locate the light switch. She stood in a narrow passage that was lit, like the outer passage with fluorescent panels along the floor. She followed the lights about ten yards and the passage ended at another doorway. Like the first, it was unlocked.

She pulled it open and mounted the stairs on the far side. Her mind whirled as she climbed. What would be the purpose of such a passage? How quickly could it be opened and someone pressed through? Who used it, and...?

She didn't need to ask herself where it led, because when she opened the door at the top, she entered a small garage. There was a black sedan parked in the center. The walls were lined with pegboards and tools. There were no windows. The far wall was a garage door, attached to an electric opening mechanism, and to the right of that was a second door. No windows, just solid wood.

She panned the phone's camera over the scene, made sure to catch the license plate, and then stopped the recording. Without explanation she sent the video to Cotter. She didn't know if he'd put two and two together, but the guy was sharp, and he'd read the story. Suddenly the disappearance of kids from this particular church had become less mysterious and a whole hell of a lot darker.

* * *

Cotter was moving before he'd even read the final pages of the story. There was simply no way that the HOA agreement he'd found in Jenifer Manske's file, and the neighborhood in the story weren't connected. He didn't return to his laptop; he went straight for his department workstation and began calling up records. He checked records of reports from that area, but there was almost nothing. He found a single report of a missing son who'd mentioned attending a party the night he disappeared, but nothing had ever been connected to the neighborhood. In fact, Cotter could find no evidence it had even been investigated.

He brought up a map and mentally matched homes to the descriptions in the story. It didn't take long to find what he was looking for. The perfect back lawn and, directly across from that, a home owned by a woman named Clarice Woodruff.

"Christ," he said. He was reaching for his phone when a notification popped up. It was an e-mail. From Teresa.

He opened it and frowned. There was no message, just a video. He clicked the link and watched as Teresa made her way through a doorway into a short passageway, up a set of stairs, and into a garage.

His mind whirled. As she'd entered that passage, he'd seen a tapestry pushed to the side. It was religious iconography, so, a church? He thought about the other story. The one where the boy disappeared on the day he was baptized.

He grabbed his phone and sent a quick text. It was

the address to the house with the perfect yard. He
added, "This is from the other story. This is the house.
They will all be watching. I am sending backup. Try
not to die."

Then he was up and moving again, running down
the hall to dispatch, and hoping against all odds that
there was at least one car in that vicinity, that they
hadn't been paid off, and that they were awake.

* * *

Teresa pulled over when her phone buzzed. She still
felt as if, no matter what she'd done, she wouldn't
have crashed, but wasn't in the mood to test the
theory. If it was true, she was a puppet, if not, she'd
probably run the car off the road and kill herself. That
wasn't going to help Pamela, or anyone else.

She read the text from Cotter, then punched the
address into her car's navigation system and peeled
out without checking her mirrors. There was no traffic
in site. As she drove, she concentrated on remembering the story, and the neighborhood. If the description had been accurate, the moment she entered that
street, she would be monitored. More importantly, the
moment she did anything remotely suspicious, there
would be a response. It was unlikely to be pleasant.

"THE WORD – REDUX"

Clara sipped her tea and shifted her gaze between

her journal, and the screens. Something had happened at Bailey's two nights earlier. Something unexpected. The unexpected was never good, and this time it came with an uncomfortable lack of explanation. There had been no meeting called. The HOA required strictly scheduled communications, but despite her friendly reminders, nothing had been forthcoming.

It wasn't the first time. There were protocols that took effect when things fell outside normal boundaries. Such periods never lasted long, but they required all hands on deck. Clara hadn't slept since the first text had failed to appear. She had jotted down every car that entered the street, every neighbor who'd ventured outside their home. She had even made notes of stray animals, mostly to help keep herself alert. She didn't know if anything she might witness would matter, but she needed the words to keep it straight.

The worst of it was the sensation of being on the outside looking in. She had her cameras, and her microphones, but they would not penetrate Bailey's place, and though she had noted others moving in and out through the garage, they did not speak. They knew, of course, that she was listening, and the distrust grated. She knew she would have to have words with Sam. There couldn't be divisions within the neighborhood. That was clearly delineated in the HOA.

A notification popped up in the bottom right of her screen, and she frowned, laying her pen aside. The neighborhood was covered by the city's network of traffic and surveillance cameras. Some of them weren't public knowledge, but the HOA had marked them. A bit of electronic trickery allowed them access to the system, but they never used it to watch. The purpose was simply an alert. When someone—anyone—accessed those cameras remotely, it set off an alert. She knew others would be seeing it as well.

She picked up her pen.

"Someone has been watching for the last few weeks. The cameras have been accessed at least a dozen times, and though Sam, and now Bailey, who has tech skills that have proven formidable, have tried tracking that access, nothing has come of it. Inquiries have been made to those just beyond our street, and we have confirmed that someone posing as various city officials, as a reporter, and as an interested realtor has been systematically gathering data on us, but with no particular focus that we can ascertain. The inquiries are random, sometimes focusing on one, or another, house. Some were about Tim, who had suddenly disappeared, leaving his mortgage unpaid and the home vacant.

"I have ordered more cameras, and I intend to request that they be discreetly installed. Not pointing at anyone in the HOA, of course, but at the perimeters, and into some of the yards and homes beyond. There has not been any more traffic than usual, and we are off of any busy route, but there was a single car that rolled through three times. It was a blue Subaru. The driver was a woman, but the windows were tinted, so I only caught an outline. I should have adjusted the cameras after the second appearance to catch the license plate, but there was simply nothing suspicious about it. Others have chosen our street as a shortcut to one business or another, and she didn't slow, or act strangely. Now I wonder."

Headlights shone on the street outside, and she stood, crossing to the window, but staying to one side out of sight.

A car was slowing, not to take a closer look, but because, from the screech of tires, it had been traveling considerably over the speed limit. It was a late model Mustang. Even with the streetlights, it was too dark to make out the driver. Clara watched it pass her driveway, and then Bailey's, slipping off into the darkness. At the far end of the neighborhood, she heard the engine rev and knew the vehicle had sped up. It was too much to ignore.

She pulled out her phone and sent a text to Sam.

"Alert 1—Mustang passing."

Then she waited. Alert 1 was code for the cameras. She knew they'd be aware, but the addition of a suspicious vehicle warranted notice. She didn't wait for a response because she knew there wouldn't be one. Instead, she turned to her journal and entered the passing vehicle.

"Something has changed. I don't have enough information to guess what it might be, but rules have been broken or ignored. Rules, and words, matter. There are no coincidences."

She laid aside her pen and rose. She needed a cup of tea, and she could see the monitors from anywhere in the kitchen.

* * *

Teresa pulled over two blocks beyond the neighborhood and grabbed her phone. She dialed Cotter and waited. It took less than a single ring for him to answer.

"Where are you?"

"I'm a few blocks out of that neighborhood. Cruised through, but didn't slow, so I only got a cursory look. I think I spotted the house that would be Clara's, and that means the next one on the right was —what—Bailey? The guy who has people in cages in the story?"

"One and the same," Cotter said. "Backup is about ten minutes out. There's no way to know what they may have in place to deal with an emergency, but if there is any truth in that story. . ."

"I'm not sure there's any truth but the story," Teresa said. "When I see you. . . when this is done. . . I want to talk to you about some strange details I've noticed tonight. For instance, does this seem a little easy?"

Cotter remained silent too long.

"Yeah, I thought so. It wasn't like this before. Or, I don't remember it being like this. If what needs to happen is that I forget all about it, I think I can live with that, but for the moment, it feels like an advantage."

"Unless we're the characters being sacrificed," Cotter said.

Teresa laughed. "No way. I'm the—what—protagonist? It's my series."

"I'm glad, then, that I'm not wearing a red shirt," Cotter said.

"I'm going back. I'm going to park in that guy Bailey's driveway, get out, and see if I can get anyone at the door. That might buy a few more minutes for whoever you have coming. I don't hear any sirens. I feel like maybe nothing is going to happen unless I'm in the middle of it, and I'm not in the mood to sit around and wait. Pamela might be in there. Or Jen. Or both."

"Maybe they're the same person," Cotter said, like thinking out loud. "I mean, you are probably someone Andrea wishes she was."

"If I find out you are having fantasies about me and Pamela, you're a dead man," Teresa said, starting her engine and making a slow turn back toward the neighborhood she'd just left. "It's not like that."

She hung up before Cotter could answer, but as she pulled away, she imagined his crooked grin.

* * *

Clara watched as the Mustang pulled back in the same way it had left. She expected it to cruise on through, but instead, it slowed and pulled into Bailey's driveway, headlights illuminating the garage door.

She dropped her pen and fumbled for her phone. Before she could send a text, there was a soft tinkle, like a bell. She opened the message.

"We see her. Watch, do not engage."

Clara's hands shook. Something was very wrong, and very strange. There were protocols. There were rules, and they were clearly written. She'd read them so many times she could recite them while watching television and not miss a beat. Bailey and the others should be removing themselves through the emergency tunnel, setting the space they were leaving to silently collapse. They would need to move, and quickly, though it would be tricky to do that without causing notice. She needed to be doing something, but she knew if she wrote any of this down, it would be dangerous. It might be found, and read, and her words were not for outsiders.

For the first time since she'd begun her first journal, she considered what a bad idea the many volumes actually were. She knew she should have installed a shredder and prepared for a moment when it was all going to hell. She'd even had a special circuit installed, because the industrial shredder she'd been eying, the one that was powerful enough to chew up and crosscut the journals, covers and all, required almost as much juice as her AC unit. The shredder had been sitting on her online wish list for almost two years, and now she wondered, if they investigated her, if that would show and be suspicious, and then whether deleting it now would still show the record and look worse.

She knew she couldn't do it. The others had their secrets, their intrigues, and connections. She had the HOA, and the words. She wondered if, without the journals, she would even exist. Not that anyone would ever read them, or even knew they existed. It wasn't in the HOA, but she was fairly certain it was the sort of thing that was an assumed rule. Don't create a string of evidence. Don't implicate your neighbors in felony crime.

The driver of the Mustang, a woman, had climbed out and was walking up the driveway toward the sidewalk leading to Bailey's front door. She wasn't hesitant. Whatever she wanted, she intended to get it.

In the distance, the faint wail of sirens rose, and Clara could make out flashing lights against low-hanging clouds. She glanced at the open journal, then picked up her pen and began to write. Absently, she wondered, if things were mostly normal again the next time the sun rose, if she could turn the stories in her journals into novels. Would the others realize? Could she use a pen name? Would anyone read them, and, if they did, how would she know?

The woman had disappeared around the side of Bailey's garage. The porch light flashed on. No one should have answered. No one should be there. Whoever, or whatever, had been in that room beneath the backyard should be buried forever in collapsed soil. Buried deep and still sealed against detection.

Instead, a wedge of light opened on Bailey's lawn as the door swung wide, and then disappeared as it was shut. The sirens were drawing nearer. Clara closed her eyes, ordered her thoughts, and then, slowly, and deliberately, she began to write.

* * *

Teresa heard approaching footsteps as soon as she rang the bell. She'd heard no sound, but assumed it was soft, or muted inside. Maybe no more than a flashing light. When the door opened, she found herself face to face with a man slightly younger than she, slim, well built, wearing chinos and a dark Henley shirt. Just for a second, she flashed on old episodes of *Dexter*, but Bailey Lawrence didn't give off a serial killer vibe. He didn't give off any kind of vibe at all. He smiled, tilted his head, looked her up and down perfunctorily, and opened the door wider.

"Yes?"

"I think you know why I'm here, Mr. Lawrence," she said. "Or should I call you Bailey?"

Sirens rose in the distance, but she forced herself to ignore them. If this man was as crazy as she believed he might be, and as dangerous, there was no telling what he might do if he knew he was cornered. And the others. Were they here? Were they closing in? She remembered the story, how Tim down the street had been taken from his own home as if he were no more than a child.

There was something in his expression that nagged at her memory. Something familiar, though she knew she had never seen him before. Never heard the name until she read it online. Bailey wasn't a common name, at least not when it wasn't the surname. She would have remembered.

"Do I know you?" he asked.

"I don't believe you do, but for some reason I have the feeling that I know you. I need to know where you're keeping her. I need to know if you have Pamela in one of your cells, who paid for it, and why. I need to get her out of here."

He stepped aside, and, heart thudding, she walked past him into the small hallway leading to the rest of the house. She stopped there. Without a word he passed her, and she followed, turning right just before the kitchen, and exiting through the open door to the garage.

It was crazy. She had only read that one story about this place, but the details felt like she'd been there a thousand times. She saw the door leading to the backyard barbecue area and watched as he worked the locks to open the hidden passage. No denial. No hesitation.

He had turned away, and she ran the short glimpse of his eyes, the twist of his lips, everything she could recall through her memory. Whatever was bothering her was recent, and important. When he disappeared down the stairs and she reached for the handrail to follow, it hit her. He was older. He had changed, but not so much, really. Not once it was out in the open.

She followed him down, but before she stepped into the room—before she committed fully—she spoke a single word.

"Jackson?"

The man stopped cold. Another surname out of order. Another impossible piece snapping into place. Just for a moment, he lost his perfect composure. It was enough.

"Why?" she asked. "Why. . . this?"

Jackson turned, face devoid of emotion, except for a slight quiver near the corner of his mouth. "I don't exist," he said. "Those I bring here? They are the same. Broken, or forgotten, irredeemable, or in need. I'm an underground railroad of the forgotten."

"No one has forgotten Pamela. No one has forgotten Jen, either. More important? Andrea never forgot you."

"I don't know an Andrea," he said flatly. "I have no one. My parents were barely aware I was gone."

"I'm not here to debate your home life," Teresa said. "I know it was bad. Do you know *how* I know? Andrea. Andrea Simmons."

He frowned. "The author? But. . ."

"Yes, the author. The author whose partner you probably have in a little cell under your backyard. The one who wrote "Shunned.""

"Shunned? That word. . ."

"I am trying to tell you, I know. She wrote your story. She wrote about the church, and your parents. She wrote about all of it, right up until you disappeared, and the story stops there. Because she didn't know. Doesn't know. She thinks you were kidnapped, killed, something. She was in your Sunday school class."

"No one noticed me," he said.

"She noticed when you were gone, so she had to have noticed you while you were there."

"I don't have anyone named Jen. I don't know who that is."

"Robin?"

He shook his head.

"Why did you take Pamela?"

"She was investigating me. She was investigating our entire neighborhood."

"So, broken, forgotten, irredeemable, or in need?"

Jackson dropped his gaze.

"This is *not* what I do," he said softly. "There are rules. There are others."

"Sam? Clara? And whatever happened to Tim?"

"How...?"

"Andrea," Teresa said. "The story was called, "The Word," and it's about how Clara watches everyone, and Tim had parties, and you built a crazy human trafficking station under your backyard. I know about the HOA. Half of the world knows about it because the story was published – under a pseudonym, and it went viral. Here's the best part. One of the two missing women, Jen, was secretly behind the website that published it. Jen is Andrea's lover.

"But there's more. After she wrote the story about this world-class sanitarium of a neighborhood, she wrote "Shunned." About you. I don't know how she connected the two, or if she did, but I know she was acting on writing prompts provided by Jen, and I think *you* know why she's missing. You want to tell me, or you want to take me downstairs and let her tell me? This place will be crawling with cops in a few minutes, but, unless the story is inaccurate, they aren't going to find us down there."

Bailey / Jackson looked dazed. He tried to speak once, then a second time, but no sound emerged.

"Now!" Teresa said.

At that moment, the volume of the sirens rose as if they'd been muffled by something that had suddenly been pulled away. Jackson moved. He turned, and Teresa followed him into the garage, watched him work the panel, and hurried down the stairs on his heels. The door closed silently behind them, cutting off the world.

The stairs weren't well lit, but at the bottom she saw brilliant fluorescent light seeping up from the room beyond and highlighting the edges of the metal stairs. In that moment she wasn't sure if she should be scared to death, angry, or wishing that it was all true —that she didn't exist, and Andrea would shortly be writing her a clever escape.

Jackson stopped at the foot of the stairs and looked

back. Teresa hurried down the final stairs and stepped into the brightly lit, almost medicinally clean room. She blinked as her eyes adjusted. There were cells all around the perimeter, but only one was occupied. She gave a soft cry and ran to the window. Pamela met her gaze and reached out, touching the glass. It was a strange, slow reaction though, as if she didn't recognize Teresa, or she was too drugged to show surprise.

Teresa stared a moment longer and then spun on Jackson, eyes blazing.

"What have you done to her? What's wrong with her? I know she can see me but. . ."

"There is nothing wrong with her. That isn't what I do. *This* isn't what I do. My assignments have always come anonymously. After Pastor Grimes got me out of that church. . . that life. . . I was sent to school. I was taken care of in private. My name was changed. My old world simply vanished.

"I've moved many times. Those who send the assignments always provide. I have whatever I need, whatever I want. When there is an assignment, I complete it with as few details and little interaction as possible. The only assurance I have ever been given is that none of those who come through my hands are innocent, or coming to harm, unless it is well deserved and absolutely necessary. Most of them are like me, forgotten, unwanted, in bad or dangerous situations.

"Things changed with Tim. It was the first time I acted on my own. The HOA saw through me. I'm still not certain how. Once I was involved, their problem and my problem were the same, and we eliminated it. Now this."

He turned to the cell where Pamela stared out at them. "All I know is that she was getting too close to the HOA. I have no destination, or pickup, because she didn't come from those who—what?—created me? I have no assurance that the others have nothing horrible in store. Everything is. . . wrong."

Teresa walked over to the glass separating her from Pamela. Something was wrong. There was no recognition in the eyes watching her. There was no sudden hope of rescue.

"Something is wrong. It's like she doesn't recognize me. I've known Pamela most of my adult life."

Jackson frowned at her. "You keep calling her that. Pamela. That's not the name of the person we took, the one who was investigating."

"What do you mean? Of course, it is. She's an investigator. I'm a reporter. She works for me."

"So, you assigned her to investigate us?"

Teresa fell silent.

"This woman's name is Jenifer Manske. She has been investigating us for a while now. At first, she wasn't finding anything, and the HOA figured it would actually be a good thing if someone investigated, and then found nothing. Something changed. I don't know what, exactly, but about a week ago, Sam and the others came to visit. They suggested. . . this. I said no. I told them it would compromise everything, that I'd have to pull up stakes and move. They were insistent, and they made it clear that, once a part of their inner circle, there was no leaving.

"Her name is Pamela. She. . ."

Teresa pressed her hand to the glass again, and the woman inside pressed hers to the same spot on the other side, but the expression was wrong. The eyes were just slightly. . . different."

"What in the hell is going on?" Teresa said softly.

She spun back to Jackson. "I know you have a way out of here. We have to get her out of there, and we have to get away without being seen."

"To go where?" Jackson asked. "They will know, and they'll find us."

"It won't matter. If we don't get her out of here, this will be the end."

"The end of what?"

"Time to find out, I think. Get her out of there."

Jackson shrugged. He pressed a couple of buttons on a control panel on the wall, and the glass panel slid back into the wall. The woman inside stumbled out, nearly falling. Teresa caught her and held her upright until she got her balance. She held the woman at arm's length, studying her face, her expressions. It was Pamela, except if she'd seen her in a crowd, dressed as she was in jeans and a tight shirt, she might have walked right past her.

"Jenifer?" Teresa said softly.

"Yes, but who. . . ?"

"We don't have much time," Jackson said.

The sound of his voice sent Jenifer reeling out of

Teresa's grip and into the wall as she realized suddenly that he was still there, and she had no idea why she'd been set free.

"Calm down," Teresa said. "We're getting you out of here. We have to get to Andrea."

"How do you know Andrea? Who *are* you?"

"If I told you that, you'd think we're both insane. I'm going to leave that explanation to Andrea, assuming we can get there."

"We can," Jackson said. "I didn't tell the HOA everything."

First, he opened an acrylic cover and pressed a large red button.

"Clock is ticking," he said. "In five minutes, this place will collapse. The others will believe I'm just covering tracks, that I'm long gone and that you are buried in rubble. The floor of the 'yard' will remain intact, but everything below will be destroyed. There are hydraulics that will compress the walls until everything is crushed. The locks will fuse."

"That's only about four minutes now," Teresa said.

Jackson nodded. He opened the panel to the cell in the back corner, then, once inside, he pressed his palm against one of the metal walls. A light blinked, and another small panel opened. He leaned down and a dim light crossed the panel, scanning his retina. The rear wall of the cell opened in the center, revealing a narrow passage beyond. Jackson stepped in without hesitation, and Teresa pushed Jenifer ahead of her into the darkness. She heard a whirring, grinding sound in the walls and did not hesitate to figure out what was making it. The tunnel ahead stretched off into the shadows, and she hurried to keep up as Jackson led them away from the hidden chamber, up a slight incline to a short set of stairs, and out onto a street just beyond the neighborhood.

"We can't get to my car," Teresa said.

"I have one," Jackson said. "I knew this day could come. We don't have to get far, but we need to get away from here before the police close everything off. If you want to reach Andrea tonight, I'm pretty sure if they find me, we're going to be detained."

"Why should I go with you?" Jenifer said.

"You published a story titled 'Shunned'," Teresa said. "I don't know who you believe he is, but this is Jackson. Jackson Craig."

"That's not. . . I didn't write that, Andrea did and it's just a story. . ."

"You might want to ask her about her inspiration when we see her," Teresa said. "Which way?"

Jackson led them down a side street and unlocked a nondescript black sedan. They climbed in without a word, and he slipped behind the wheel. Moments later they were rolling slowly away from the neighborhood and turning onto a main street, with traffic, lights, and people. The world had never seemed more surreal.

* * *

Cotter was standing by dispatch, waiting, when the call came in that they were moving in on the house. A description of Teresa's car was all he needed to hear. His shift had been over for more than an hour. He stopped by his locker on his way out and grabbed his service weapon. His job didn't involve arrests, or chases. He was there to find hidden answers, line up the clues, and take the photographs. It didn't change the fact he was an officer, that he'd come up as a rookie like the rest, before completing the courses necessary to move into the crime lab after hours. He hadn't fired the weapon anywhere but the gun range in over a year, but he felt that if there was a time he needed it, this was that time. He didn't bother to bring his belt and holster. Didn't want to draw any attention on his way out. He was thankful for the earlier storm, because he'd worn a jacket with pockets big enough to conceal the weapon.

He hit the parking lot at a slow jog, slid behind the wheel of his truck and hit the streets. He didn't even slow down as he hit the street. There was nothing he could do at that house, and there were plenty of officers there if something went down, but he had an idea that there was an entirely different place where things were coming to a head, and he intended to be part of that.

* * *

Jackson pulled into the driveway of Andrea's home, and the three of them got out. Teresa started up the steps, but Jen hesitated.

"What?" Jackson asked. "This is the place, right?"

Jen nodded. "A lot has happened since I last saw her. I don't know how she'll react. I don't even know how to feel."

"Trust me," Teresa said. "She is frantic. I spoke with her earlier today. She's been freaking out ever since you disappeared. Tell me, though, does she know you published those stories? Does she know you were behind the writing prompt site?"

"No."

"And you didn't know about Jackson, but you published the story. You didn't know it came from her past? Didn't bother to check the name of the pastor online?"

"Even if I'd thought of that, there was no time. The e-mails and investigations, even threats, had started to pour in from the first story, and I was scared. I mean, it's just a story, right?"

Jen shook her head. "I've been publishing that webzine for a while. I didn't want to tell her because I wanted to do it on my own, not as the assistant, or lover, to a famous author. The writing prompt site was something one of my readers suggested. Just a way to use a sort of creepy format to get the creative juices flowing. It was never meant to be serious. I didn't know she would take it so seriously."

"And you weren't already researching the HOA when you did all of this? You didn't know?"

"No, of course not. She wrote that story a couple of weeks back, and it freaked me out. I went through our HOA here, and it was like I was obsessed. You never think about things like that, and it was so creepy. It was when I started searching for other agreements that I noticed similarities to her story and that other neighborhood. It was creepy. Very secretive, and, when I drove through it, there was a party going on at that house. . . right where the story said it would be. I thought I saw someone in the window across the street and thought about that woman. I never went back, but I started asking questions and collecting information, thinking Andrea might have known something, or someone, and that I could, I don't know, help?"

Jackson stared at her, and she turned away quickly.

"A couple of weeks? We took Tim three days ago."

The two stared at one another, brains trying and failing to align the pieces.

"I think we'd better get inside," Teresa said. "I wouldn't try too hard to make sense of time just now. It seems a bit. . . fluid."

She turned and continued onto the porch, and the others followed. Behind them, in the distance, lights flashed, and the whine of sirens echoed through the night.

The door wasn't locked. Somehow Teresa had known it wouldn't be, but at the same time, hoped that it would. The hallway inside was just as she remembered it. She waited, but when Jen didn't show any signs of taking the lead, she started walking toward the lighted office at the far end.

No one called out. No frantic footsteps, no greetings, or questions. As they neared the office, Teresa heard the steady clicks of fingers on a keyboard. At the threshold she stopped, glancing in. Andrea was leaning over the desk, hair askew, typing. It wasn't a headlong rush, but a very steady flow. There was a rhythm to it, and with a soft gasp, Teresa felt it matching the beating of her heart. At that gasp, the typing sped, then slowed, and stopped.

Very slowly, Andrea raised her hands from the keyboard and turned the office chair around, staring at them. Teresa crossed the room and looked past her to the screen, scanning the last few lines. Her heart sped again, and, out of the corner of her eye, she saw Andrea's fingers twitch.

"What. . . the actual fuck?" she said softly.

On the monitor, the last words that had been typed glowed softly.

"There was a rhythm to it, and with a soft gasp, Teresa felt it matching the beating of her heart. At that gasp, the typing sped, then slowed, and stopped."

The others gathered around, read over her shoulder, then stepped back. Jen held out a tentative hand to Andrea, who shook her head, as if disconnecting from some thought, or dream. She took the hand and rose shakily into a tight hug.

After a moment, Teresa spoke.

"I hate to interrupt the reunion, but now what? What about me? What about Jackson?"

Andrea extricated herself from Jen's arms and turned. She started to speak, but before the words could form, they all heard the click of the door closing down the hall, and the sound of approaching footsteps. They all turned to the door.

Cotter stepped into the room and glanced around. He had his phone in his hand, and he glanced down at the screen.

"What is it?" Teresa asked. "How did you get here? Why...?"

He held up his phone and she crossed the room quickly. The screen was filled with text, as if he were reading an eBook. The last words on the screen were the same as those on the monitor behind her.

"This makes no sense," Teresa said. "We are still here, still talking and moving, but the words ended. Where does that leave things? And, by the way, since this is apparently the Jen you have been writing about, where exactly is Pamela and why does Jen look exactly like her?"

"She's the key," Andrea said. "She has always been the key. Jen, Pamela. . . I never realized how thoroughly I based one on the other."

Turning to Jen, she continued. "I have always known you wanted to write, to be out there, doing things and making a difference, but I'm selfish, you know? You have always been here for me, and I was certain if that changed, if we were any less close, and I had to start relying on myself, either I would fall apart —or you would leave. So, I created Pamela.

"She is independent. She collaborates with Teresa but is not tied to her. She has a life, a future, and it's how I imagine you might have been. . . without me."

"You say all of that as if she doesn't exist," Cotter cut in, "But I've met the lady. She is a top-notch investigator. I've also met her fiancé."

Andrea smiled wearily. "I was already afraid Jen would catch on to what I was doing with the character. If I'd made her life into any more of a parallel to hers, there would have been no way to deny any of it. Giving her a fiancé that rarely shows up during the events of any given novel was enough to remove any desire I might have had to entangle her with Teresa in any romantic way."

Teresa frowned. "I'm not. . ."

"I know," Andrea said. "I am, though, and Pamela is based on Jen. I never really based you on anyone in my life. You are someone I thought I would admire, someone with characteristics I like to think I have, but probably don't. My adventures all happen right here, at this desk in front of a keyboard. My life, particularly my thoughts, are a mess most of the time. You are always sure of yourself. You don't hesitate. You speak your mind. If it seems as if someone needs to know something, you tell them. I wasn't even able to tell Jen I was worried I was stifling her, because I was afraid of what she might do. I know that's stupid, but the best I can do most of the time is to write it down. I have actually stopped myself when confronted with something I didn't want to deal with and imagined how I would write you handling it."

"You never had to worry," Jen said. "I'm not here because you smother me, you idiot. I'm here because I love you."

"I know," Andrea said, "but I also knew there were things I simply wasn't part of. I sensed it, and it frightened me. And now I know it was this. Your writing, the webzine, and your own stories, a whole network of people and words I knew nothing about. And the prompts. How did I end up on that page? You didn't tell me about it. . ."

"I left clues," Jen said. "I left magazines open to articles with writing prompts. I responded on social media every time I saw one. I even tagged you in some of those, trying to spark your interest. When you felt like you weren't really creating, that you needed something new, I hoped those would stick in your head, that you'd remember all those prompts and look for a new one. If you had never found the site, I'd have been more direct, but you did."

"What if I'd said no?" Andrea asked. "What if that line had appeared, 'Are you a talented writer?' and I'd simply said no? Or I don't know?"

"Exactly what happened when you said yes," Jen replied. "It's just a simple program. It has one function, to get you to the first prompt. Behind the scenes it drops that writing sample into an AI bot and returns a random prompt with a time limit. The time limit to complete the assigned prompts is also random, though the first is set to twenty-four hours by default. There is nothing sinister in the code. There was nothing personal, or magical about it. It treats all entries the same."

"Does it?" Teresa asked. "I went to that site, you know. You must know, it's probably recorded somewhere in that document," she waved at Andrea's monitor. "I typed a sample, and was given a one-word prompt, and twenty-four hours."

"Redemption," Andrea said softly.

"Yes, that is what it said. It made no sense to me then, and it makes no sense to me now. I'm a journalist. I don't make stories up, I record them."

"We both typed those words," Andrea said. "When you went to the website, I was there with you, channeling whatever it is that connects me to you, and to the story. I typed the word redemption..."

"Why?" Cotter cut in. "Whose redemption, and from what?"

"That's what it's been about all along, isn't it?" Andrea said with a shrug. I set out to prove I'm not a hack, that I didn't get derailed and sent off into formula fiction land by comments from a childhood friend. That I wasn't ruining the only relationship I have that has any real meaning to me. That I have something to say and have been saying it. I have no more idea how I set all of this," she waved her arm vaguely around the room, "in motion than any of you do. As usual, though, I was self-indulgent to the point of cutting off everything and everyone, even those only trying to support me."

Jackson, who had been silent the whole time, finally spoke.

"So, this is redemption? I'm the only one here with literally no idea who the rest of you are beyond the fact you and I may have known one another in Sunday school years ago, but I have to say, I don't see it. What has been redeemed? Rather than straightening out your life, it seems you have pretty much trashed ours?"

Andrea blinked. "Isn't it obvious? I might have been writing formulaic novels for a very long time, but this time—whatever all of this is—is something more. However, I did it, my words brought all of us together in this room. You," she pointed at Jackson, "and your crazy neighborhood probably exist here, and in the words, because I remember you. I remember that church, and how sad it seemed that no one ever spoke to you. I remember the day you disappeared. I had blanked it out, like kids do, but that's one of the reasons I write. To dig out those hidden bits and pieces of my past and work through them."

"That doesn't help me any," Teresa said, "Or Cotter here, or Pamela. Does she even exist now? Is she gone forever? When I drive home, where will I be, and will this house still be here? A place I could visit?"

"I don't know yet," Andrea said. She turned away and sat at her desk. She typed a flurry of words, and as she did, Teresa's phone chirped. She had an incoming message.

She pulled the phone out and stared. "It's from Pamela."

Cotter hurried over to her. "What does it. . .?"

At the desk, Andrea continued typing, drawing it all in on herself. Jen stood and watched, just for a moment. She leaned down and kissed Andrea on the head. "I won't wait up," she said.

Andrea nodded, but she was already gone, barely aware of the transition. As Jen left, she closed the door as quietly as she could.

Teresa turned toward the door, taking Jackson by the arm. Cotter followed. He glanced back one time, but the room had grown fuzzy. He tried to concentrate, to remember what he'd been thinking, but moments later they were on the porch and headed for Jackson's car. As they pulled into the street, his thoughts shifted to the message from Pamela, and what would come next.

* * *

As she concentrated on the words, reaching for new threads to pull them along, Andrea pictured their faces. Jen, Teresa, Cotter, and Jackson and she thought, *You are all here with me, and I need you as much as you need me. I live in two worlds, and when you leave. . . I disappear.*

ACKNOWLEDGMENTS

I would like to thank my better half, Trish, for putting up with my constant babbling about this book, and for its first solid edit. Ute Orgassa, for her early comments. Ai Jiang, Ray Garton (who we lost shortly after he read this) Linda Addison, Clay Mcleod Chapman, Steve Rasnic Tem for being gracious enough to read advance copies and offer blurbs. James Orestad for the title, the posting of which broke the block that was preventing me from finding the ending. Robin Orestad for being a good sport and lending her name to a main character. Nancy LaFever and Erin Foster for their editing work. And the twelve cats of Stately Wilson manor for only sometimes preventing me from typing.

ABOUT THE AUTHOR

David Niall Wilson is a USA Today bestselling, multiple Bram Stoker Award-winning author of more than forty novels and collections. He is a former president of the Horror Writers Association and CEO and founder of Crossroad Press Publishing.

His novels include *This is My Blood, Deep Blue,* and many more. His most recent published work includes the novel *Jurassic Ark*—a retelling of the Noah's Ark story... with dinosaurs—and his collection, *The Devil's in the Flaws & Other Dark Truths*. David lives in way-out-yonder NC with his wife Patricia and an army of pets.

A NOTE FROM
SHORTWAVE PUBLISHING

Thank you for reading! If you enjoyed *When You Leave I Disappear*, please consider writing a review. Reviews help readers find more titles they may enjoy, and that helps us continue to publish titles like this.
For more Shortwave titles, visit us online...

OUR WEBSITE
shortwavepublishing.com

SOCIAL MEDIA
@ShortwaveBooks

EMAIL US
contact@shortwavepublishing.com

ALSO AVAILABLE FROM SHORTWAVE PUBLISHING

ALSO AVAILABLE FROM SHORTWAVE PUBLISHING

ALSO AVAILABLE FROM SHORTWAVE PUBLISHING

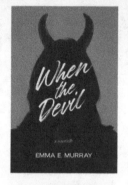

ALSO AVAILABLE FROM SHORTWAVE PUBLISHING

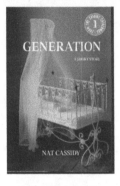
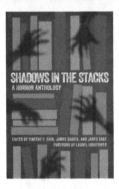

Printed in the USA
CPSIA information can be obtained
at www.ICGtesting.com
JSHW031029180524
63152JS00005B/23